CROWN ME YOURS

HEARTSTRING DUET
BOOK TWO

LIV ZANDER

INK HEART PUBLISHING

CHAPTER
ONE
A WORD OF CAUTION

This is a dark fantasy romance, containing situations that might make some readers uncomfortable. You can visit www.livzander.com for details, or reach out to me directly! info@livzander.com

TWO

Elara

We wrap the dead with our hands steady and our mouths shut while the afternoon sun hangs bloody over the palace graveyard, casting long, distorted shadows that stretch toward the open maw in the earth.

Mother and I lift the king from his bier. Not a gilded thing, not a carved coffin fit for songs; just a plank of wood laid across two trestles, because even royalty runs out of ceremony when rot has eaten the world's appetite for pretending.

Kael is lighter than his height and stature suggest, hollowed out by years of carrying a curse. Mother's arms still tremble, harder when she looks at me, then up at the golden spikes fused to my skull.

"Legs," I say, just to cut the silence. My voice sounds like gravel, mostly unused since I crowned myself dead in the throne room yesterday, since Death vanished in a whirl of shadows and rage.

"I've got them," Mother whispers, voice cracking.

A shroud covers Kael's face, clean linen pulled tight enough that the shape of his nose makes a small ridge, the hint of his mouth a soft dip in cloth. It feels wrong that I can't see him. Wrong that I'm relieved I can't see the slash across his throat.

I adjust my grip under his shoulders, his body cooling rapidly in the autumn air. Stiffness clings to his joints, that rigor that gravediggers know intimately, the body's final stubborn refusal to bend.

We lift him onto the lowering straps. Practiced. Efficient.

Mother reaches into the woven willow basket at her feet. Dried marigolds. Bright, orange, cheerful, offensive little things. She takes a handful and arranges them around the shrouded head. Another handful, larger this time, she lines up across his neck.

Mother watches her wrinkly hands work and slowly shakes her head. "To hide the blood that crusts in the fibers."

The petals settle, masking the angry red grin I carved into his throat. A mercy for the observers. A lie for myself. If you cover the slash with marigold, maybe it's just a garden, not murder.

Maybe.

Something knots between my ribs, tightening with each breath, gaze going to those sunken hollows where Kael's blue eyes would be. Daron is best with the eyes. He would have been gentle with them, carefully sliding the spoons under the lids. Instead, my brother lies in his bed in the west wing, rattling and gurgling, too weak to attend a king's funeral.

A restless shuffle draws my eyes up from the grave. A handful of people stand in a semicircle. Two priests in white robes that look too clean to be holy. A scattering of courtiers gather behind them, looking like they're watching a play they don't understand.

Neither do I.

Miss Hampshire stands apart from them, her hands clasped tight over her starched apron. She keeps glancing at the crown on my head, the gold biting into my scalp with the patient insistence that it belongs there now. It doesn't slide when I lean, doesn't shift when I swallow. It sits fused to my skull, part metal, part bone, a pulsing thing that only moves when I lift it with my own hands.

"This is improper," one of the priests mutters, his face like risen dough, his eyes darting nervously to a palace guard stationed nearby. "A king's funeral rites ought not to be carried out by a...a new *queen*."

The last word comes out like he scraped it off the bottom of his shoe—thick with contempt, edged with disgust for women who dare touch things reserved for men.

"A queen just the same," I say, my voice flat. "The dead don't care which hands lower them, so long as they land soft. And nobody drops them softer than a gravedigger. All that shoveling numbs the arms. No choice for us but to handle the body with care."

He bristles, his pious indignation fading behind narrowed eyes. "This is a disgrace."

Mother exhales, slowly and funneled. "Elara," she whispers, voice thin as a hair. "What...have you done?"

I straighten, wiping my hands on the black mourning silk Miss Hampshire found me in a forgotten wardrobe. It's a habit. A reflex. "I did what I thought I had to."

"That is not an answer."

"It's the only one I have for now."

"The people will be outraged," the priest says, louder, looking into the half circle of people in support. "A common gravedigger woman wearing the crown? It spits on the royal bloodline. The monarchy is built on tradition, not... not dirt under—"

"You have been in the chapel for too long, Father." It is Miss Hampshire who speaks up, her voice dry as old parchment, cutting through the priest's sputtering. "You forget the smell of the streets."

The priest blinks, his doughy face slackening. "I beg your pardon, Miss Hampshire?"

She lifts her head, and the pustule above her brow catches the fading sun, shiny and defiant. "The realm has been rotting for years. Children eat mud; mothers eat their stillbirths." She looks at me then, her gaze sharp, assessing, but not unkind. "The common folk won't care if she digs graves, so long as they don't get rolled into them. They will only care," she continues, her voice rising just enough to carry over the wind, "that there is a new ruler who might yet end this rot."

The priest opens his mouth to retort, perhaps to cite some scripture about the sanctity of royal blood, but he looks at the crown and closes his mouth. He steps back, defeated by a housekeeper with missing fingers and a queen with dirt under her nails.

I look at Miss Hampshire, at the ally I least expected, then back at Mother before I give a nod. "I'll take the shoulders."

Mother takes the feet. Her eyes are wide, glassy with unshed tears, but her jaw is set in that line I know so well—the line that means we have a job to do, and we will do it until it's done. We grab the straps.

Kael is unwieldy the way dead things are, weight pulling toward the earth, eager to return to it. We shuffle to the edge of the hole I dug this morning. The soil is dark and rich here, fed by generations of mostly royal decay.

We lower. The straps hiss against the wooden supports as Kael descends into the dark, black earth. It's a sound I know better than my own name. Friction of rope on bark. The soft, inevitable *thud* as the body finds its final bed.

The strain in my forearms grounds me, calming the screams in my head into the honesty of gravity. Death is simple.

You stop breathing. You get heavy. You go down.

There is a comfort in the finality of it.

The palace graveyard is quiet, but not peaceful. Trees, tall and clipped, their shadows long and thin. The stone markers are carved with names that once mattered enough to be chiseled. But rot doesn't care about names. It eats everything just the same.

Including Daron.

Beyond the graveyard fence, the palace walls loom—wet raven slate and sweating stone, the air still carrying that faint vinegar stink they use to pretend the sickness can be scrubbed away.

Farther still, the city squats under a haze the color of decaying leaves. Smoke from a thousand small fires smears the horizon. Hunger doesn't stop because a king dies. Rot doesn't pause to see who wears the crown now.

"I'm sorry," I whisper, the words catching in my throat, too low for the people to hear. Most of them are already turning away anyway, not seeing the single tear that tracks hot down my cheek. "What am I supposed to do now?"

A pat on the back is all the advice Mother can offer before she, too, turns away. "Time to look after your brother."

I look after her for a moment, gaze catching on those dark veins on her neck. Aside from that first telltale sign of rot, she's asymptomatic, but for how long? How many days, weeks, or months until rot will show on a finger? A toe?

When the first shovelful of dirt hits the shroud, Miss Hampshire steps up beside me, black dress starched to cracked whiteness at the seams, cap pulled low. "He was a good man."

"Was he?" I watch the dirt cover his hand—the hand that had held mine in the spring, that had trembled against my cheek. "I can't help but feel like I knew nothing about him. Nothing."

She shakes her head, watching the grave fill. "I know he was fond of you."

The words land soft...

...and still, they split me.

My throat tightens until swallowing feels like dragging cloth through a wound. I keep my face still—queen-still, gravedigger-still—while my insides lurch like a cart wheel hitting a rut. *Fond...*

He'd been cruel and stubborn and half-mad with hope. He'd kept his secrets locked up like coffins, so tight that even when he shoved the crown onto my head, he couldn't spare a breath to tell me what I'd become. And yet...his hands *had* trembled when he touched my face.

I stare at the dirt swallowing him inch by inch and feel myself pulled in two directions. One part of me wants to spit on his grave for leaving me with this mess. The other wants to claw the earth back open to shake answers out of him.

It doesn't matter. He's gone because my hands did what they do best: deathwork.

"What am I supposed to make of all this?" I turn to Miss Hampshire, the early evening sun now slanting through the trees, turning the fresh mound of dirt into a golden smear. "Did he mention anything? Leave instructions? Anything at all?"

She shakes her head, watching the footmen work silently, rhythmically, the spades slicing the earth. "He came to me that morning like a man possessed," she whispers. "Eyes wild. Shirt unbuttoned. He looked...terrified. And hopeful. He told me to prepare for the rite, and that is what I did."

I watch her profile. The lines around her mouth are deep canyons of worry. "Did you know he would make me queen?"

"No, not until..." She hesitates, stalling until the footmen carry off the spades. "Our best hope to break the curse. That is what he called you before he sent me to ready the knife."

"But how?" I all but breathe.

"I...I do not know. He kept his counsel close, Ela—Your Majesty." A solemn dip of her head. "He kept me in the dark, same as you. Only the dead know now. And the messenger."

"What messenger?" The one I saw in Kael's room? Someone else entirely? "What's his name? How can I find him?"

Miss Hampshire's mouth works as if she's trying to grind the right words into shape and finding nothing but grit. Her half-hand lifts, nubs flexing once against her apron before she clamps it there again, fingers she no longer has curling into the fabric. When she finally meets my eyes, the silence she offers lands in my gut like a stone.

"So he just crowned me clueless..." The familiar sense of defeat sinks its teeth into my ribs. If I don't figure out what I'm supposed to do, the curse will keep eating the realm— and Daron will be its supper. "For all we know, that messenger might be dead, too."

"Perhaps."

She curtsies—a stiff, formal dip that looks ridiculous given the situation, given that I am standing over a fresh grave with dirt on my shoes. It's a gesture of manners, a desperate cling to order in a world that has dissolved into chaos. Then she walks off.

Only the silence stays with me, descending onto the graveyard as the sun finally dips below the horizon. It bleeds a vivid, violent red into the gray sky for a bit, until twilight deepens and swallows it whole. The air grows cold, smelling of damp earth, wet stone, and the promise of winter.

I remain by the grave until my legs ache, staring at the dirt. This is where I belong. Not on a throne, not in a palace. No, I belong among the silent and the dead, and the decay that whispers through the headstones.

"It's about ending it at the source," I whisper as a few tears slide down, warm and furious, dripping onto the thirsty grave. "What the fuck did you mean?"

A wind picks up, rustling the dead leaves around the headstones. It swirls the mist around my ankles, cold and biting. It carries a familiar scent, so at home at a graveyard. Not rot, not earth.

Carnations.

My spine stiffens, a million goosebumps pebbling my skin as memory flashes before my mind. Moonlight. Bone. Black pits where eyes should be. A ribcage that held a rumbling moan in lieu of a heart.

"You have a nasty habit," a voice says behind me, smooth as oil and cold as the grave, "of fighting me like I am not inevitable."

THREE

Elara

I don't turn around immediately. I let the wind bite my cheeks and the scent of turned earth fill my nose one last time, grounding myself against the sudden, cloying smell of mourning flowers. When I do turn, he's leaning against the gnarled trunk of a tree.

Not Death. Vale.

Twilight catches the sharp line of his jaw, bringing out the tense shift of muscles there. Arms crossed over a chest clad in midnight-blue velvet, he looks exactly as he did the day he stepped between the headstones of my family's plot —arrogant, impeccably groomed, annoyingly handsome.

A devastating facade.

"Dressed up for the occasion, I see," I say. "Doesn't the costume feel a bit tight around the shoulders?"

Vale's green eyes narrow slightly on the fading light tracing the horizon, then they find mine. "I prefer a form that doesn't send mortals screaming into madness. It simplifies...conversation."

I step away from the fresh grave, the hem of my funeral cloth dragging heavily in the stiffening grass. "Why bother? I've seen what's underneath the silk."

"I daresay you haven't just seen it." His mouth twitches. Not quite a smile, not quite a snarl. "You have also...felt it."

I don't flinch.

I refuse him that reaction.

The memory ignores my refusal. It crawls up my legs, a phantom frost settling high on my thighs where his hands had been. I remember the shock of ivory gleam, a construction of bone and decay that had thrust into me with agonizing pleasure.

I shove the thought into the dark place where I keep my screams. "One less reason to keep up the pretense, then," I say. "What shall I call you from now on? Lord Death? Just Death?"

"I am quite fond of *Vale*."

"Obviously," I grind out, waving a hand at his too-shiny black curls, his too-perfect face. "Why not take him off, hmm? Why not show me your true form?"

His eyes flick over me. Not the way a man takes in a woman, but the way he measures a problem. They linger a beat too long on my mouth, though—perhaps on the slight tremble there—then drop to the grave mound.

"Presume," he finally says, "that the way you screamed, fled, cowered, and hid under a table serves as a perfectly adequate reason."

Heat flares under my collar, hot and sharp, burning away the lingering cold. I hate that he saw me reduced to a scrambling, terrified child, hiding from the very thing I've spent my life burying.

"I'm sick of the fucking masks." I take a step toward him, forcing him to look away from the dirt and back at me. "Do it. Drop the theater. If we're going to talk, I want to talk to the thing that created the curse sitting on my head, not the pretty puppet it used to seduce me."

"Seduce you?" He pushes off the tree, moving with that fluid, determined grace that screams predator, no matter how fine the velvet that wraps it. "If I recall correctly, Elara, then you came to me." His voice drops, shedding the polite veneer for something darker. "You came to my room," he murmurs, stopping inches from where I stand rooted. "You pressed those small, gravedigging hands against my chest and practically *begged* to be ruined."

My breath hitches, traitorous and loud in the quiet graveyard, but I hold my ground against every instinct screaming to run. "I came for instruction."

"Is that what you're telling yourself?" A smile touches his lips, slow and wicked. He reaches out, a finger tracing the line of my jaw. "Do not rewrite history because you're frightened of the ink, little queen. I remember the way your pulse hammered against my mouth. I remember the way you unraveled." He lowers his head, his lips hovering beside my ear, his breath a cool whisper against my skin. "I remember how you sounded when you came on my cock."

My knees weaken. The heat of him—or the cold pretending to be heat—radiates into me. Flashbacks hit me like physical blows: the slide of silk falling away, the arch of my back, the guttural sound I made when he filled me.

"Stop," I whisper.

It isn't a command. It's a plea.

He ignores it. His thumb brushes the hollow of my throat, finding the frantic beat of my pulse. "If anything, *you* seduced *me* with your...blatant disregard." He catches my wrist, bringing my palm up to his mouth, his lips grazing the calluses earned from the shovel this morning. "You move through the architecture of my existence with such ease. You stand in the center of my domain, amidst the worms and the decay, and you look so perfectly, *terrifyingly* at home."

The tension snaps tight, gravity pulling me toward him while my body flushes with unforgivable tingles. Until my eyes drift past his shoulder. To the mound of dirt.

Tingles turn to a death chill.

I reach up and grab his wrist with the force of a woman who hauls dead weight for a living and yank it away. "You're mistaken."

He blinks, the seductive haze faltering. "Am I?"

"When I came to you, I came to *Vale*," I hiss. "Because I was starving for anything that wasn't death." I drop his hand like one drops a corpse. "Don't mistake my desperation for desire, you lying, scheming *monster*."

The temperature plummets until frost crystals bloom on the grass beneath us with little *clinks* and *clangs*, the remaining curve of his mouth straightening into a line so thin it's almost invisible. Something startlingly human flashes across his eyes before it's swallowed by an abysmal anger.

"Says the biggest liar of them all." His voice drops, losing its human cadence, vibrating against my ribs with ruthless force. "How about we drop this farce, and you simply tell me what it is that you demand."

What I demand of him? Why would he think I have any leverage...

"What?"

"Oh, please. You and Kael? Quite the performance." A brittle scoff slips out of him, terrifyingly bemused. "Out of sheer curiosity, at what point did you two decide to collaborate against me, hmm?" The words are almost conversational. Until his hand snaps up, fisting in my hair at the scalp and yanking my head back, letting pain prickle across my scalp. "Was it when I was gone dealing with that foolish little farm girl? Was he whispering promises about your brother's life if only you'd spread your legs like a good little whore, letting Death fuck you?"

I wince, about to deny it, but his other hand grips my chin, forcing me to look at him.

"And the curtain... Oh, the curtain!" he shouts. "That stroke of theatrical genius. Kael's suggestion, wasn't it?" He laughs, a sharp, humorless bark. "Come to think of it, you must have plotted it that night, after I left you shivering beneath the table. Oh, how cunning. I left as you demanded, and you..." He stops, his expression twisting, something ugly and raw breaking through the nonchalant veneer. "You ran right to him, and I was left the fool once more."

For a heartbeat, I just stare at him while my mind scrapes itself raw against the echo of his words. "*When a mortal fools Death,*" his voice drifts from our past, "*Death must grant a wish.*"

Something lifts inside my core, the meaning of those words clicking into place with the same cold certainty as rigor sets into bones. But of course! To him, it must have looked rehearsed—Kael crowning me, shoving the knife into my hand, timing the cut while Vale was a step too late.

Given the chaos of all that transpired since the greenhouse, he's convinced that Kael and I had plotted this all along. That we cheated him.

That I fooled Death.

Which isn't true. Not at all. If anything, I was about as clueless as him, but I'm not so stupid as to confess that. If Death's humiliation buys me a wish, I'll damn well take it!

I stop fighting his grip, stop trembling. I let a cold, gravedigger calm settle over my face—the kind I use when the grieving scream at me for things I can't change.

"Took you long enough," I say.

Vale freezes, releasing me. His rant dies in his throat, pupils blowing wide as he searches my face for the lie and finds only the hard surface of my resolve.

Then he scoffs, the last of twilight gleaming off his black curls. He rakes a hand through them, a gesture too mortal, gaze going to the horizon once more before he looks back at me.

"I didn't know what to make of what I was witnessing until the very moment you opened his throat." His jaw works, the muscles bunching tight beneath the skin. "It's no small confession for any man to admit he's been made a fool, yet it's a particular humiliation for me, when the laws that bind me do not allow my foolishness to pass unpaid." Tilting his head, he shifts nearer, his eyes narrowing on my lips for the shortest moment before they find mine. "What, Elara, is it you demand of me?"

"How can you not know what I demand?" My wish requires no thought, no consideration, that excitement expanding at my core a guiding force. "Lift the curse. Destroy the crown and take your damn heartstring back."

"Denied." The word is instant.

"What?" That expansion in my chest comes to a halt, shriveling under the pressure of a forced inhale. "You just said—"

"The crown exists because of a wish—made by a king long forgotten, protected by laws mortals cannot fathom." Vale steps into the space I'm trying to defend, his nearness a suffocating weight. "Did you really think it would be that easy? That you could simply wish away centuries of debt with a single breath?" He dips his head, his lips grazing the shell of my ear, his voice a mocking caress. "I cannot grant a wish that directly contradicts a prior binding."

My chest tightens, the hope that had flared just seconds ago brittling into ash. I want to slap him, pound my fists against that velvet coat, but I force my arms to remain by my sides. Anger is useless if it's blind.

Think, Elara. Think.

What do I demand?

"Interesting," he murmurs, eyes narrowing as if he's trying to read the thoughts inside my skull. "I expected a quick, calculated demand, oh-so perfectly arranged by the late King Kael. Or is it possible that he was so busy scheming, he forgot to tell you what ought to come next?"

My pulse throbs inside my ears, but I refuse to let it reveal my ignorance. I could ask for Daron's health to be restored. For his lungs to clear. For the color to return to his cheeks. Just a few weeks ago, that would've been my wish. But that was before Mother arrived at the palace with dark purple veins, rot spreading silently beneath her skin...

"Tick-tock, Elara." Vale's hand slides up my arm, his thumb drumming into the pulse point that betrays my growing panic. "Night is coming. Even I do not have all of eternity to wait for you to make up your mind."

"I won't let you rush me," I snap, jerking my arm from his grip. "Can I...can I wish for my family's health to be restored?"

Something loosens in his stance—a tension I hadn't realized he was holding until it evaporated. The corner of his mouth ticks up, not in a smile, but in a look of supreme, insulting pity.

Like...like I asked the wrong question.

"You might as well ask for the health of the entire realm, and that contradicts what this fabulous crown demands in return for its existence." He steps closer still, until I have to tilt my head back to meet his gaze. "But I shall make a concession for my *lover*," he purrs. "Daron, or Mother?" His eyes are alight with amusement, watching the wheels turn in my head. "Choose, and I shall restore his or her health." He brushes a stray hair from my forehead, his touch lingering. "But only once."

Only once...

Because rot remains and might claw its fangs into my family all over again. Daron could wake up healthy tomorrow, only to wither again by next harvest, and I would have spent my one bargaining chip on a temporary bandage for an eternal wound.

"I have other matters to attend to, you know," he murmurs. "People are dying in droves. Watching you dawdle makes it difficult for me to tend to the souls piling up." His thumb strokes along my lower lip, slow and intimate, but my breath doesn't hitch until his mouth dives for it. For a sick, disorienting second, it looks like he's going to kiss me, only to tilt at the last moment and press his mouth to my ear with a faint chuckle. "Five...four... three..."

His stupid countdown sharpens my mind like a whetstone. He's trying to confuse me. Rush me. Trying to get me to make a mistake.

My throat narrows.

I can't demand the curse away. My family's health is a fickle wish. I'm trapped in a cage of rules I didn't write, playing a game I don't understand. Kael left me nothing: no instructions, no guidance.

Whatever he thought I could do to break this curse, he took it into the dark with him. What am I supposed to do? Take matters into my own hands? Wait around for a messenger who might never come?

My gaze snags on the mound of fresh, damp earth. Kael knew something. Something that could break this curse. If I had five minutes...just five minutes to wring the truth out of him...

I look up, meeting Vale's smug, expectant gaze. "Can you bring him back?"

The smirk slides off Vale's face. He blinks, the casual, leaning posture of his body stiffening into something rigid and terrible. "Bring him back," he repeats slowly.

"Kael," I clarify, my voice trembling but gaining volume. "Do you have the power to resurrect him?"

He stares at the grave, and then at me. His expression twists into something concerning. Something petty.

"You want *him* back?" His voice drips with disdain, and beneath it, a current of searing heat. "Why would you want him breathing again?"

There's no answering that in any truthful way without revealing that this bargain stands on a lie. "My reasons are my own. Surely sharing them isn't a requirement for you to pay up."

A symphony of brittle cracks echoes through the graveyard as the grass beneath us turns ghostly white. The frost doesn't just coat the blades, it entombs them; the chill shooting up through the soles of my boots, biting through the leather with stinging numbness.

Before I can stumble back, Vale's hands snap up to bracket my face. The grip is ruthless, his palms pressing against my cheeks with the weight and finality of a coffin lid slamming shut, trapping me in the cold with him. He lowers his forehead until it rests against mine, the contact burning like ice, his eyes searching mine with a terrifying, fractured intensity.

"Pathetic." The rage in his voice cuts the air like sleet. "You stand before Death, owed a wish that could topple fate itself, and you ask for the return of *him?*" His eyes darken. "Was he your lover, Elara? Did you let him put his hands on you after you denied mine, hmm? Is that why you wept on his grave? Did his death break your stupid, mortal heart?" His thumbs press until flesh meets molars. "Do you love him!?" he roars, the sound vibrating through the soles of my feet. "You stand before a god, and you pine for the rotting flesh of a man?"

Fear rips through me so hard it rattles my lungs, stealing the air in a jagged pull. For a moment, I'm nothing but bone and breath trapped between his hands, my pulse hammering against his palms while confusion whirls through my skull.

The way his thumbs dig into my flesh, the wild, wounded accusation, the way his eyes blacken under the rising moonlight with sheer possessiveness—none of this is the reaction of a god fooled.

It's the jealousy of a lover scorned.

No, impossible. He cannot love. He has no heart to give and apparently, no wish to get its string back. So, whatever this is, it's not tenderness.

It's arrogance. It's ownership.

It's possessiveness that tries to make me shrink, tries to control me. And I'll be damned if I let myself be bullied by his stupid, wounded pride.

I lift my chin against his grip, forcing my breath back into my chest, and meet his gaze. "Can you bring him back or not?"

For one heartbeat, he just stares at me, wide-eyed, as if the strike of my question could make even a god bleed. Two seconds. Three. The pressure of his hands increases until my teeth ache. Then, as if he realizes what he's doing—what he's showing—his grip breaks.

His hands fall away.

The cold rushes in where his touch had been, and I draw a harsh, greedy breath that stings my throat. Vale turns from me sharply, shoulders rigid beneath velvet, as though the sight of my face is suddenly too much to bear without losing whatever thin mask of composure he has left. He rakes a hand through his curls. Smooths his cuffs. Stares past the headstones into nothing.

When he finally speaks, his voice is stripped of all emotion, a hollowed-out echo of the man who was just shouting in my face. "No."

"No?"

He doesn't look at me. His gaze fixes on a sliver of moonlight cutting across the frosted grass, right beside his boot. "Even if I were inclined to grant such a waste...Kael has been cold for hours. He has been dead too long."

My heart gives a violent lurch. *Too long.* Not *impossible.* I step toward his back, unable to stop myself.

"But that means..." I trail off, my mind racing. "That means it's possible? You can bring someone back?"

He doesn't answer. He doesn't even acknowledge the

question. He simply turns around, his face smoothed into a strange blank mask, the rage of a moment ago buried beneath layers of ancient, impenetrable ice.

"What is your wish, Elara?" he asks, clipped and cold, as if he had not just stood here with his hands on my face and rage in his throat. "Choose it. Now."

The demand hangs in the air, a blade waiting to drop, but my mind is a whirl. Every wish I conjure—health, wealth, power—feels like a mistake I refuse to make.

My silence seems to unnerve him. He shifts his weight, agitated. His boots crunch on the frozen grass as he takes a step to the left, then another to the right, pacing.

No, not pacing.

Dodging.

The clouds above are thinning, tattered rags revealing the rising, blinding face of the moon, and beams of silver light are beginning to pierce the cemetery canopy like spears.

Something shifts in my stomach. Earlier, he refused to show me his true form, and now the moonlight is slowly stripping him of that defiance. Why, I don't know—whether shame, or pride, or something else altogether—but it'll buy me time.

I simply do nothing.

I stand and wait.

"I am failing to see the complexity here," Vale snaps, the vibration of his frustration crackling in the air between us. He lifts his hand, leveling a finger at my face to punctuate the command. "Speak the words, Elara, or I will rip them from your—"

The wind kicks up, tearing the final rag of cloud from the moon's face. A beam of silver light hits him mid-threat. It strikes his outstretched hand, and the illusion doesn't just falter, it evaporates, elegantly tapered fingers dissolving to sinew and bone.

He freezes.

Vale stares at his hand, at the skeletal claw protruding from the rich velvet of his cuff, stark and horrifying against the night.

He jerks his hand back as if burned, clutching it against his chest. "Next time, little queen."

Vale spins on his heel, the velvet of his coat seeming to lose its solidity, melting into the surrounding darkness. Shadows curl around his boots, rising like smoke, weaving through his form until he's nothing but a smear of ink against the night, vanishing completely and leaving me alone in the silent, freezing dark.

FOUR

Elara

Daron breathes like someone poured soap water into his lungs and forgot to drain it. Each inhale is a wet rattle, each exhale a thin, exhausted pop that makes his ribs show beneath the blanket like a cage struggling to hold in life.

I sit on the edge of his bed and pretend the damp cloth I press to his forehead is making a difference. We both know it's not. "Hang in there just a while longer."

How long, I have no idea. Weeks? Months? Every time I seem to take a step closer to breaking this curse, fate strips days from my brother's life and seemingly turns them into new hurdles for me.

What do I demand of Death?

"Broom queen…" Daron struggles his eyes open. "You smell like…dirt."

"I've been around it."

He tries to smile and fails halfway, pupils catching on the gold rimming my forehead before they disappear behind wax-pale skin again. "Always wearing that thing now."

The crown on my head hums faintly as if it enjoys being mentioned. It bites where my hair parts, a constant reminder that no matter how I sit, no matter how I lie down, I'm tethered to this mess.

I could give it to Daron.

Crown him king.

The thought has been chewing my guts since last night, since meeting Death in the graveyard. If I place this thing on his head? Put the knife in his hand? If he slits my throat and bleeds me over the crown in one swift, deep slash?

The idea is so hungry it almost tastes like hope. Until he winces, blue-veined lids trembling, struggling to open, only to fold under pain.

If he can barely lift his lids, what are the chances that he can lift a knife? And I'm not allowed to help with the rite— that much I remember Kael saying—rendering this idea as useless as all the others. Unless I demand Death restore his health?

That still leaves Mother rotting, though, the wish potentially wasted. If I swap the roles? Crown Mother queen, and wish for Daron's health? But then we're back to Daron potentially falling sick again.

My arms turn heavy enough to make my shoulders

ache. No matter how I twist and turn this, there's no true solution. It also goes against what Kael wanted...whatever the fuck that might've been.

"Elara?"

I jolt, blinking away the various contemplations of my own murder. "I'm here, Daron. Right here."

He tries to turn his head, a grimace of effort twisting his lips. "Itches," he rasps. "Cannot...reach."

"Where? Where does it itch?"

"Behind...the ear." He tries to lift his hand.

I watch, breath held, as his wrist trembles. The tendons strain, his knuckles turning white with exertion, but his hand lifts a fraction of an inch off the mattress before gravity reclaims it with a heavy, lifeless *thud*.

A chill sweeps through me.

No, he can't do it.

"I got it," I whisper, forcing my voice steady. "Let me see."

I lean forward, gently moving his sweat-dampened hair aside. The skin behind his ear is inflamed, a dark, angry purple. I touch it lightly with the damp cloth, intending to soothe the itch, but the moment the fabric makes contact, the skin moves.

No. It slides.

A layer of wet, gray flesh sloughs off onto the linen, revealing the raw, weeping meat beneath. The rot isn't just in his lungs anymore; it's eating its way out of him.

"Just a bit of dry skin." My stomach lurches violently. I swallow the bile, my hand shaking as I toss the cloth onto the floor. "I need... I need to get the comfrey salve for that. It's in the infirmary, but I'll be quick."

Daron merely grunts.

I rise before the anxiousness in my stomach becomes

too heavy, and hurry from the room. The hallway is silent this morning. A lantern flicks in a wall sconce, throwing thin light over my skirts as I hasten along the runner rug before I pass doors, nooks, more doors. Once I take care of Daron's wound, I'll still have to check on Mother, see if—

A hand clamps over my mouth, a hard, brutal seal that stifles my scream before it's born. An arm, rigid as steel, hooks around my waist. With one hard yank that lets air whoosh from my nose, someone pulls me into an alcove of tapestry and shadows.

Heart pounding, I thrash. "Mh-hmm!"

Heels kick at shins.

Fingernails claw at leather.

"Quiet, Your Majesty," a voice hisses in my ear—rough, urgent—and the hand tightens over my lips until my teeth threaten to shatter. "Quiet, or Kael died for nothing."

The man hauls me backward through a narrow door, into darkness that smells of mildew and old stone. The door shuts right before my eyes. My feet scramble, *plop-plop-plopping* down a spiraling stone staircase. Deep. Deeper.

Darkness presses against my eyes, black and absolute, the stench of vinegar replaced by rust and damp earth. Until the man finally stops and releases me.

Flint strikes. Sparks hiss.

"Who the hell are you!?" I scramble backward, back hitting the damp stone wall, fingers digging into the mortar to the sound of a torch sputtering to life. "What do you want from me?"

"Please, Your Majesty, lower your voice." He brings the torch between us, letting the flame skitter over thick brows, a sweat-slicked forehead, cropped hair as brown as his mud-streaked travel leathers.

"I know you." Not by name. By memory. "You're the messenger. The one who came into Kael's room that day."

"We cannot stay here." Torch in one hand, he wraps the other around my arm, pulling me over slick stone. "Walk, Your Majesty. Walk with me."

"What? Why? What do you—" Stone shifts beneath me, letting me stumble over a rock, arm flailing for balance while a rat squeaks somewhere and skitters into the dark. "Where are we going?"

"Nowhere, so long as we keep moving."

"Why?"

"Stillness is like a bell that Death can't unhear," he says over his shoulder, not slowing as he guides me along chilled cellar walls, barrels, mounds of stone where they crumbled from the ceiling. "It's the nature of the grave to be still. His senses are more likely to drift to us if we linger."

The sheer conviction in his voice—the palpable terror coating his words—makes my feet catch up before my brain agrees with that logic. "Why did Kael crown me queen? What am I supposed to do? He said you'd come. He said you'd explain."

"I would've found you quicker, but I couldn't take the risk of Death finding me out first." He takes a sharp left that leads us into a wider cavern that smells of old wine. "As Kael's only confidant, I'm complicit in undoing this fucking curse, and Death would torture that knowledge into silence if he knew my identity. Name's Corvin, Corvin Hale."

"Break the curse, how?" I press, ducking under a low archway. "Nothing makes any sense!"

"Shh..." Corvin's eyes flick over his shoulder to my crown, and something bleak shifts in his expression. "He wasn't lying... It truly took," he murmurs, as if to himself. "You're the first queen to wear that crown longer than a few seconds, you know. The original translation of the curse was changed to *son*, not *heir*. *King*, not *ruler*. Priests scrubbed the language, swapped consort for bride, and sealed it into tradition so the curse would travel through men and men alone."

Original translation. I reach up, touching the cold metal of the crown. "Kael discovered the changes."

"One of his pigeons brought me a note the day you slit his throat. Hastily written, barely legible, demanding I seek you out. Said you mentioned the bloodline was impure already, and he found proof of that, too." A scoff. "Can't believe we wasted a year tracking down a distant cousin about a dozen times removed."

"The farm girl."

"Aye." He casts a nervous glance at the shadows pooling between empty wine racks. "Kael believed that crowning her queen would finally pave the way to breaking the curse." He shakes his head, resuming his frantic pace. "I was careless. Stayed in one place too long."

My throat narrows. "What happened to her?"

"Who knows? When I returned with supplies...the house was ice. Just ice. She was gone." A shrug. "She's irrelevant now. Destroying this devilish crown is a task for a queen. For you."

I stumble over uneven flagstone, first beads of sweat gathering on my nape. "How?"

When we turn into a corridor that smells like wet iron and old piss, his steps slow, bunched brows frowning back at me. "The note also said that he thinks Death took you as his lover. That true?"

My steps falter, slowing us further as heat floods my neck, letting a single pearl of sweat run down my spine. "I... It's true."

Corvin falters to a halt. For a heartbeat, the only sound is water dripping somewhere in the dark and the faint, exhausted hiss of my breath. His eyes hold mine—sharp, disbelieving.

"Saints..." It's not so much a whisper as it is a faintly breathed laugh. "Not even rumors exist. In a thousand years of lore, not a single sound about Death taking a lover. He's solitary. Rarely touches the living unless it's time to reap them."

Shame claws at my throat, heated memories of Vale's naked body flashing like a bruise pressed too hard, but it's drowned by a harsher need. "So I was told, but I still don't fucking know what to do with that. What does it change? I'm still carrying a cursed crown. My brother is still rotting."

"When Kael put that darned crown on your head, he changed the debtor to a *woman*," he says, gaze drifting to nothing behind him before his eyes find mine again, the flame of the torch letting hints of gold ripple across his brown eyes. "Now, Death's lover carries the curse, and—"

He winces, eyes frantically darting to a glistening sheen of sweat on the wall. A fine white crust creeps outward from the edge of the wet patch, spidering over the mortar in delicate veins. The torch flame shifts, bending away as if a mouth just exhaled in the dark. Cold, sharp and sudden, slides under my skirts—not from the floor, but from the air —biting straight through wool and skin until my knees prickle and my teeth threaten to chatter. Then I smell it.

Carnations.

"We have to go." Corvin's fingers dig into the flesh of my arm once more. "We stopped for too long."

He yanks me forward again, faster now, making me stumble a few steps before I manage my strides. We pass rusted bars that line one side, prison cells, doors hanging open like mouths. A chain hangs from one door, black with age.

"The crown is a magical binding, demanding a debt to be paid," he huffs, pulling me toward a stairwell that spirals upward a short distance, faint light casting down on it. "But what happens when the curse gets fed with the blood of the creditor?"

The scent of Death fades slightly, or perhaps it's the burn in my lungs fooling me. "I don't understand," I pant. "You want me to feed Death's blood to the crown?"

"Not just that, but complete the entire rite. Come on." He shifts behind me, hand releasing my arm and wandering to the small of my back, herding me up the tight spiral as if my body is the only door he can slam between us and what we're running from. "Up this way, Your Majesty!"

The stone stairs sweat harder beneath my soles than my armpits do, slick and warm, and with each turn the air thickens—less piss and iron, more damp heat, like breath trapped under glass. A wet gust hits my face, heavy with loam and something mellow. Sap. Leaves. Growing things.

The torchlight dies behind us, and a pale, sudden brightness spills down from above, so abrupt I blink hard, eyes stinging as my pupils scramble to adjust. Green flickers; yellow-speckled leaves clinging to life, blackened stems, a tangle of branches that scratch against iron trellises. Dirt crumbles beneath my heel. My breath catches. Glass glows. Condensation weeps. Where...?

I squint into the light, and my stomach turns over. "Is this—"

"Queen Maeryn's greenhouse, yes. Your Majesty..." He steps in front of me and drags a breath deep enough that it makes his chest rise. His eyes flick once to the panes above

—too much light, too exposed—then back to me. He scrubs a hand over his stubbly jaw, the words stumbling as if they're reluctant to be born. "If...if he's got a body, he's got blood. If he's got blood, it can be spilled. And if that blood touches the crown while the rite binds you together...then the loop closes. The curse shatters."

The words land like a punch. "The rite? But how—"

"Coronation," he blurts. "Making Death your consort is our only hope. Your Majesty, you have to...have to..." Another deep breath. "You have to wed him. Bed him. Crown him. Then slit his throat and bleed him over the gold."

An unexpected bark of laughter rips out of my throat, sharp and hysterical, bouncing off the glass panes. My head spins, the scent of damp soil and warm greenery suddenly cloyingly rich, turning my stomach. I stumble back, hitting a potting bench hard enough to rattle the clay pots stacked there.

"Wed him? Bed him?" *Again?* "Put the crown on a god's head and then slit his throat?" The sheer, towering absurdity of it makes the world tilt, the condensation-streaked glass above swirling into a kaleidoscope of gray sky and rotting leaves. "This is madness."

Corvin looks at me, unblinking. "Kael was certain. He had spent years unrolling scrolls, finding hidden translations to unravel the roots of this curse."

I grip the rough wood of a bench just to stay upright, breathing through the sudden wave of nausea that threatens to purge my meager breakfast. "This is too much. It's too—"

Corvin's gaze snaps past me to the glass panes above, to the drifting gray light, to the condensation shivering, as if the greenhouse itself has begun to listen.

"He desires you. That's leverage. Use it," he says. "I have to go."

"What?" My grip tightens on the bench until my knuckles blanch. "You can't just drop a theology of impossible tasks at my feet and leave!"

"There's too much information to be tortured out of me, and the less we appear to know, the less threatened he'll feel," he throws over his shoulder, boots whispering over damp soil before he shoves past a trellis. "There's no more I can do here."

"He already knows what Kael tried to do, or he wouldn't have gotten rid of the girl!" I hurry after him, half stumbling, skirts catching on a thorny branch. "How am I supposed to achieve any of this?"

"In the same manner you managed to seduce Death." He reaches a portion of wall swallowed by ivy so thick it looks like a rotting curtain, digs his fingers in, and wrenches it aside. Behind it, a narrow door reveals itself, iron-banded and old. "Consult the scriptures if you must."

"He was furious at my coronation." My breath comes too fast, dragging dense warmth into my already exhausted lungs. "He was in my face last night, shouting and snarling, so it's safe to say he hates me!"

"His hate is not your greatest hurdle," he throws over his shoulder, voice rough with urgency as he fumbles a key ring from his belt. "Yours is."

Those last words land in my stomach before I can even process them, my mind still stuck on wed, bed, crown, slit —on the absurd choreography of it. "My hate?"

He stutters a key into the old lock, letting the door grind open on age-old rust. "Love. You have to love him."

Another sharp laugh scrapes out of me, more breath than sound. "Impossible."

He squeezes himself through the gap. "Good luck, My Queen."

"Corvin—"

The door howls shut.

The plant curtain draws.

I don't move for a long moment. I simply stare at the trembling ivy, dumbfounded, the greenhouse humming with damp life struggling to survive. Water drips from a leaf. A thorn clings to my skirts. Somewhere above, a cloud darkens the already gray sky.

Something shifts at my core.

So this is what it takes...

Love aside, if I approach this sequence backward, it appears doable. I look down at my hands, calloused from shovel handles and grave dirt. Fuck, I'd love to drag a blade over Vale's throat. Put this crown on his head? Be my guest. And bed him? I've done it once. Twice. Kind of. I can do it again. But how does one convince Death to become your husband?

My lips twitch into a smile.

No, not convince.

Demand.

CHAPTER
FIVE

Elara

Fog clings to the lower graveyard like a shroud, blanketing the servants' grounds, so thick it beads on my lashes and turns the world into smudged silhouettes: crooked stones, stunted yews, a slanted fence. And the two men lifting out a grave in the distance.

It's the hour between worlds—the gray, damp seam in time right after dawn breaks—where the silence is so heavy it feels like pressure against the eardrums. Any stiller, and I might as well be dead...

Sitting on the frost-damp grass, I watch the spades cut

into the earth with practiced rhythm, dark soil piling into a mound. One man puffs white breath into the sky. The other wipes his brow, casting a pitying glance back at me, at the queen in the dirty dress who's been sitting here a long while. How much stillness does that bastard need to finally show himself?

When the men shoulder their spades and leave, my gaze drifts to the pink-streaked horizon. I made sure I came here at a good time, with the moon faded and dawn bringing enough light for Death to hide his bones. Was he truly that gruesome to look at?

I squeeze my eyes shut, reaching for the grotesque memory. What I find feels softened by time, the terror of it strangely blurred. Skin pallid like a corpse's, yes, but also smooth and flawless. Ribs exposed for certain, a body stripped down to its simplest truth. Is there a heart behind them? And if I somehow ever manage a glimpse, am I going to find it with its strings ripped to shreds?

I sigh.

Wed him. Bed him.

Does the morning in the tower count? When I pulled the curtain? Or was that just lust with no intent? I don't know, but I can't risk a technicality. Lying with him is probably a step in the right direction under the circumstances.

I stand, my knees popping in the cold. I cross the lower graveyard and walk up to the edge of the fresh hole. Dug for a kitchen maid, I overheard one of the men mention earlier. Poor thing didn't even die of rot. No, she took a tumble down some stairs and snapped her neck. Pity.

The scent of loam and worms rises from the grave, its familiarity letting warmth settle under the cotton of my dress. I hitch up its skirts. My boot toes the edge, finding a foothold in the clay, and I slide down.

My soles hit the bottom with a soft *thud*. Walls of earth rise above my head, cutting off the view of the trees, the path, the everything, leaving nothing but a rectangle of gray sky above.

It's colder down here.

Much colder.

I lie down, the back of my dress soaking up the dampness. Hands crossed over my chest, I am so still, forcing my breath into something dead-shallow as I stare at the sky. *Come on now, you asshole...*

Nothing.

No scent of carnations. No chill sliding under my skirts. No shadow thickening at my feet. No—

Crunch.

The sound is slow but deliberate. A boot on gravel. Then silence. Then another crunch. Closer.

I don't breathe. I don't blink.

Dirt rains down from the edge, a gritty sprinkle that lands on my cheek. A shadow blots out the gray sky. Vale leans over the lip of the grave, his black velvet coat absorbing the mist, his hair a dark halo against the morning light. He looks down at me, brow arched in supreme, unimpressed boredom.

"Feeling theatrical, Elara?" His voice is a low rumble that vibrates in the narrow space. "Or have you finally realized where your sense of fashion belongs?"

My molars grind back a scathing comment about the fashion of tendons dangling from bones. "I was waiting for you."

"In a hole? Things that cannot be killed hardly belong in graves. It's bad luck."

"I was told you like stillness."

"Oh?" He tilts his head, a predatory gleam entering his

eyes. "I must say, I liked the way you rolled your hips against me much better."

Without warning, he jumps.

I gasp, instinctively flinching as he lands beside me, his coat brushing against my arm, the scent of carnations and ice instantly overpowering the smell of the dirt.

And then he lies down.

The narrowness of the grave forces him to press against me, arm to arm, leg to leg. A gravedigger lying beside Death in a kitchen maid's grave. Hysterical.

I turn my head. Vale's profile is sharp, pale as marble against the dark earth wall. He isn't looking at me; he's staring up at the sky, his hands folded over his stomach, mirroring my pose.

"Make your wish," he says softly. "I have places to be."

I watch the slow, steady rise of his chest. "I'll make you a deal."

He snorts. "You don't have the currency for a deal."

"Show me your true form," I say, ignoring his arrogant bemusement. "Let me see Death, and I'll make my wish."

The easy arrogance evaporates, replaced by a cold rigidity. He turns his head slowly, and this close, I can see the tiny flecks of gold in his irises.

"You demand your wish, and I grant it," he says, his voice dropping. "That is the transaction. I do not perform parlor tricks for your amusement."

"It's not amusement. It's…" Curiosity, probably, but that seems too morbid to confess. "It's…knowing who I'm dealing with."

"You're dealing with the end of all things."

He turns back to the sky, dismissing me. But he doesn't leave. He stays there, the heat of his body—yes, heat—seeping through his clothes into mine. It's strange. For all the coldness he can bring, near me, he sometimes seems to burn like a fever.

We lie in silence for a long moment. It's surprisingly peaceful. The wind howls above us, but down here, shielded by the earth, it's quiet.

"Why didn't they see you?" I ask quietly, breaking the truce. "In the city. At the Gutter Lane house. My mother, Daron... They all looked right through you. But the kitchen girl...she saw you."

Vale sighs, a sound of weary patience. "I am a concept, Elara. Even in this form, most minds refuse to perceive me."

"But I saw you. I saw Vale."

"Because I chose to let you see Vale," he murmurs. "And once the curtain is lifted, it cannot be lowered. Not in this form."

I nod in understanding. The kitchen girl saw him that night because he'd appeared to her before. No wonder she was scared. She didn't see a steward or even a prince; she saw Death.

"The carriage driver who brought me here." My mind wanders back to how he asked if I was alright. How Miss Hampshire mentioned the next day that talking to myself was not permitted. "He never saw you, did he? Probably thought I was mad."

"What else would you call a woman who cozies up in a grave beside Death?" Vale shifts onto his side, turning to face me just in time for me to see a twitch leaving his jaw. "Enough of this nonsense." The annoyance in his voice is sharp enough to scrape. Vale's eyes narrow, not in anger—*not yet*—but in that bored, predatory way that says he's about to stop indulging me. "I didn't climb into a grave to trade memories of carriage drivers. Ask what you're clearly prepared to ask, Elara, before I decide you're wasting my morning."

The scathe in his voice pricks at me. The distance between Vale's patience and his rage is unpredictable at best, but maybe I can still risk more questions? Learn about the power he wields and the rules that bind it?

I roll onto my side, leaving nothing but an inch between our faces, warm breaths mingling in the air. "The farm girl. Kael's *distant scrap of blood.*"

"What of her?"

"Did you kill her?"

"This again?" Again that shift in his jaw, barely there, but I catch it. "I cannot take a life like that."

"You told me as much, but who knows?" I shift in the grave, the movement sending a small cascade of dirt down from the grave's edge, but it mostly sprinkles on him. "You're Death. It's in the title."

"Do you really think I busy myself with mixing poisons or pushing old men down stairs?"

I look at the dirt on the velvet of his collar, Corvin's voice murmuring through my skull. *He desires you. Use it.* My pulse rises into my throat, but I simply let it pound there. Death is a man, he said so himself, and I now understand what it takes to seduce one.

After all, *he* taught me.

I reach out, fingertips slowly brushing the dirt off his collar. "If it suits your plans."

Vale hesitates, eyes narrowing, flecks of gold catching in the gray light. "I am not a plague. I am not a blade. I am not the hand that pushes a child into a river." His voice turns colder. "I am merely the one who collects the soul."

Daron's soul, and that thought drives a shiver along my arms. "You're making yourself sound pretty innocent, considering you created a curse that's killing thousands over the death of one ferryman. Even if he was your friend."

His jaw clenches and unclenches. "Innocence is a mortal invention...as is guilt. I don't decide how much sand is in a mortal's hourglass—though I might tap it a little."

I slide my fingers from his collar to the sharp line of his jaw, feeling for stubble where I only find polished river stone. "Tap?"

Vale's throat works once beneath my hand, a swallow that shouldn't matter and somehow does. His pupils flick to my fingers on his jaw, then slide back to my eyes with that lazy, infuriating calm he wears when he's deciding whether something will be amusing or merely tedious.

"I can...*nudge*." His exhale comes with the slightest weight pressing into my fingers, almost as if he's sinking into my touch without wanting to make it too obvious. "Hours. A day. Rarely more. I can stretch a fraying thread a little, or pull it taut so it snaps sooner—if it was going to snap, anyway."

In an instant, images of a cherry-red splotch running down porcelain skip before my mind. "The library scribe."

"He was so close to his end, it took minimal effort." His tone is bored, but his body isn't. Not with how his breathing quickens the longer I trace his jaw. "I merely made a slight...adjustment."

Adjustment. I file the information away, alongside the hint that he can probably bring back the dead. Every limitation he admits to is a crack in an armor I'll eventually have to pierce.

I slide my touch to his cheek, letting my thumb trace the corner of his mouth. "What happened to her, then? The farm girl."

"What happened to her is that she will remain a farm

girl," he murmurs, his gaze sliding to my lips before it finds my eyes again. "And you will remain queen in her stead."

The words land too neatly, too knowingly, to be casual. *In her stead.*

My thumb stills at the corner of his mouth, and for a heartbeat, the grave feels even narrower, the air thicker—because that's not the language of a god who stumbled into a trap. Kael may have fooled him in the throne room, but Vale is not stupid. Oh yes, he knows exactly what Kael meant to do.

What *I* am meaning to do *in her stead.*

I trace my fingers up along his cheek, slow enough that he could stop me if he wanted. He doesn't. He lets my fingertips find his hair, those too-neat curls damp at the roots from the fog. I comb through them gently, then my fingers drift to his mouth, thumb tracing his lower lip.

He stays perfectly still, allowing the touch, but a dark, taunting smile curls the corner of his mouth against my skin. "Trying to distract me from that wish, little queen?"

"Is it working?" My thumb pads at his bottom lip like one would at a blade to test if it cuts, fingertips tingling with how fast my pulse grows. "Maybe I'm just curious."

He chuckles, but there's a mean, vicious edge to it. "Curious."

His hands shoot up, clamping around my wrists with bruising force. In one fluid, terrifying motion, he wrenches my arms up, pinning them into the dirt on either side of my crown. He rolls, his weight crushing the air from my belly, his hardness pressing against me.

"Curious!" he spits, the amusement gone, replaced by a gaze that burns cold enough to freeze blood. "Or cunning?" He dips his head, his nose brushing against mine, his voice dropping to a lethal whisper. "Do you think I don't know what you're doing? The *seduction.* The *luring.*" He tilts his head, his lips hovering inches from mine, tantalizingly close. "You think you can beckon me into your bed and make me vulnerable enough to bleed over that crown? Little queen, I won't give you the reaction you seek."

I buck my hips. It's a brazen, reckless move, grinding the center of me straight up against the hardness straining beneath his trousers. "I don't know, but something sure is reacting."

"A biological imperative," he snarls, pressing down harder to stop me from moving, which only increases the friction. "A flaw of the human form. Do not mistake this as any progress on your goal, Elara, for I could fuck you right here, and it would merely be an itch scratched."

"Then do it," I challenge, lifting my chin. "Scratch the itch."

He stares at me, chest heaving, sense warring with sensuality. "Infuriating woman!"

He crashes his mouth down on mine.

It's not a kiss. It's a collision.

It's teeth and tongue and a hunger so ancient it feels like it might swallow me whole. He devours me, his grip on my wrists tightening until I'm sure I'll have bruises in the shape of his fingers. I kiss him back with equal desperation, arching into him, using the slide of our bodies to fuel the fire.

We grind against each other, the wool and velvet creating a maddening barrier.

This better count...

"Has it occurred to you," he pants, his voice rougher with each grinding stroke, "that your *beloved* Kael was wrong? That whatever fairytale logic you depend on is nothing but the hopeful scribbles of a desperate man?"

For a split second, doubt blooms cold in my chest. What if he was wrong? What if I'm debasing myself, stripping my pride raw in a muddy grave, for a solution that doesn't exist? But then, why is he so damn angry?

No, this is the way.

I yank my hands free. Before he can stop me, I shove my skirts up. Cool air hits my thighs, followed by the searing heat of his weight. I reach between us, my hand fumbling with the fastening of his trousers.

"Elara..." he warns, but his hips betray him, pushing forward into my hand.

I only get two buttons undone. It doesn't matter. I shove my hand inside, fingers wrapping around the velvet-hot steel of him. Come on...

"I want you inside me." I tug, struggling against the tight fabric, managing to free only the head of his cock before the waistband traps him again. "Please."

He groans, a broken, desperate sound as his head drops, his resistance crumbling. "No..."

I lift my leg, hooking it around his back with a yank toward me. "Vale..."

"Damn you, Elara!" He rubs the exposed head of his cock against the damp silk of my undergarments, finding the seam, finding the friction. "Fuck..."

"Inside!" I cry out, frustrated, bucking up, trying to capture him. "Put it inside!"

Vale humps me more frantically, a rhythm born of pure, unadulterated need. It's messy and desperate, the friction searing through the thin fabric. I claw at his coat, trying to pull him down, trying to force the alignment, but he's too strong. Too fucking stubborn.

He slams his hips against mine once, twice, harder—

And then, with a guttural shout, he unravels.

I feel the heat of it, wet and sudden, spilling over my stomach, over the cotton, soaking into my underdress, but never touching the inside of me. He shudders, his forehead collapsing onto my shoulder, his breathing loud and harsh in the quiet grave.

He lifts his head, looking at the mess between us—the wasted seed pooling on my skin. And he laughs, a dark, dry sound.

He rises, adjusting his clothing, leaving me exposed and sticky and unfulfilled. "Close," he whispers, the mockery returning to his eyes, though they're still glassy.

I shove my skirts down, fury igniting in my chest like a flame tossed onto straw. "You fucking bastard!"

"Hardly." He straightens his coat, chin adopting an arrogant tilt, and turns to place a boot on the wall of the grave. "You gave me permission to scratch an itch, so I scratched it."

"My wish!" I shout when he readies to hoist himself up, leaving me covered in the proof of his mockery. "Is for you to marry me!"

Vale freezes. His boot slides off the clay. He stands there, staring at the wall of dirt mere inches from his nose. Slowly, painfully slowly, he turns back around. The mockery is gone. In its place is a stillness so profound it feels like the air has been sucked out of the grave.

"What?"

"You heard me." I scramble to my feet, ignoring the dampness clinging to my body, the trembling in my legs. "You will become my husband."

The air crackles. The temperature drops ten degrees in a heartbeat, frost instantly blooming on the roots protruding from the grave walls.

"You *dare?*" Vale's face twists, his lips curling back from his teeth. "Of all the things you could ask for—gold to fill this pit, an end to your brother's pain, perhaps even a resurrection once he finally rots—you try to chain *me?*"

A jagged line of darkness splits his cheek, revealing the gleaming white of a skeletal jaw. The green of one eye doesn't just darken; it rots away, dissolving into a hollow socket. He flickers—man, Death, man—as if his godly rage can't be contained by human skin.

"I will not bind myself to a mortal!" he roars, the sound letting dirt rill off the walls. "I am eternal! I will not play house with a fleeting spark of life that will burn out before I even blink!"

"You have to!" I shout back, fear warring with a wild, desperate hope. His hostility...it's too much. It's too defensive. If marriage meant nothing in this, he would laugh. He would agree and let me age and die while he watched, bored.

But he's *furious.*

"I refuse!"

"You can't refuse!" I step into his space, chest heaving, adrenaline flooding my veins. "Does it interfere with another wish? No! Does it break the direct wording of the curse? No!" I shout, breathless. "Does Death keep his word?"

He flinches. The supernatural rage falters, hitting the immovable wall of his own rules. The black fades from his eyes. Pallid skin weaves over bone.

Then, a cruel, twisted smile slices across his face.

He leans in, his lips brushing my ear, cold as the grave itself. "Fine," he whispers, the word a scratching sound against my skin. "I grant your wish. I will marry you." He pulls back to look at me, and the malice in his gaze makes me want to scream. "I will play your husband for twenty, maybe thirty *miserable* years. I will watch you wrinkle. I will watch your beauty rot. And when that last kernel of sand finally drops"—his hand comes up, gripping the back of my neck, not tenderly, but like a master claiming a hound—"I will take your soul, and I will drag it down to the deepest, darkest pit."

CHAPTER
SIX

Vale

Somewhere in this realm, a dam burst mere hours ago, flooding the lowlands. Currents are sweeping through rotting families, letting an avalanche of souls tumble into a void where they cry out for direction. And what is their guide, the darker half of the universe, doing?

Getting *married*.

Standing beside an iron sconce inside this old chapel, adjusting my white cravat as I suppress a groan at this farce. What a waste of a perfectly good Tuesday.

I look down at the rope tied around my chest. A symbol of union, the scrawny priest behind the altar explained, but all that coarse, primitive thing does is destroy the fine velvet of my umber coat.

Wed him. Bed him.

Slit his throat and break the curse.

I shift my weight, the stone floor hard beneath the boots of my mortal form as I wait for my…wife. Does Elara really think she can end the curse with this lunacy? Chain me with a ring on my finger, and save the remnants of her brother's life?

The thought is almost adorable.

But only almost…

My chest clenches as it often does when I think of her. Had Elara been sensible, she would have wished for her brother's health. Then she could have chosen a mortal man whose nature doesn't leave her shivering under a table. A mortal to put a child in her belly with excitement rather than fear, securing her succession before she kills him to feed the crown.

A man she can love.

Images flash before my mind, unbidden and vivid. Elara smiling up at some faceless noble, her hands tangling in strands that aren't mine. Blond, probably. A kind man. A wholehearted man.

A man I can never be for her.

Something curls beneath my ribs, strange and sudden. Not pain exactly. More like a stretching, a tightening.

Utterly foreign…

I look down at the culprit, at that damned ceremonial cord strapping down my lungs. I roll my shoulders. Exhale hard. Then I expand my chest with a deep inhale, fighting the trapping sensation.

It doesn't yield.

It cinches relentlessly against my sternum, forcing my breath into something shallow. The pressure draws attention to what lies beneath: not a heart of muscle and valves, but hollow numbness and scar tissue clinging to the remnants of my heartstrings.

Torn. Forever broken.

Exactly how it needs to be.

I lean against the nearest column, arms crossed, and glance back at the priest. "How much longer can this possibly take?"

"Her Majesty is almost ready," someone says, who is most definitely not the lanky priest, his face unmemorable in the way most mortal things are.

I turn my gaze toward the voice.

Miss Hampshire walks into the chapel with two candles and a tight mouth, that aura around her still pulsing with a vigor that started to bore me too many months ago. That woman just won't die...

She pauses when her gaze crosses mine, recognition narrowing her eyes. "Good morning."

I scoff. "Is it?"

Miss Hampshire doesn't flinch. It's a quality of hers I always respected, earned over decades of service to blood-crowned kings and slaughtered queens.

She moves to the altar, placing the candles in their proper places, adjusting cloth, setting out a braided cord— all ceremonial nonsense—with what's left of her hands.

A soft scrape of shoes on stone pulls my attention to the chapel doors. A woman's. *Elara's mother.*

She enters quietly, wrapped in a plain shawl that has been mended more times than it has been washed, hollow eyes immediately finding mine. When she stops in front of me, she doesn't hint a bow, doesn't fidget, doesn't do what sensible peasants do in palaces. She simply looks, long and slow.

For a heartbeat, my veil tightens over my true nature, as if the way her aura dims with each blink frays the edges of my illusion, letting her see who will come for her soul soon enough. But there's no fear, only an unknowing recognition that pricks even at my patience.

Finally, her wrinkled mouth parts. "You look like a man who doesn't sleep."

Indeed, and it's her stubborn daughter who's to blame for it. "Work keeps finding me endlessly."

Mother hums as if she expected as much. "Elara has always had work, too," she says. "Even when she was small, she'd rather carry a bucket than play with dolls. Always hauling something heavy, like it was her birthright." Her mouth curves. "When she was upset, she'd go sit among the stones behind our home. Said the dead listened better than the living."

A faint tremor runs through my hands, so slight I'd deny it if anyone could see. I don't like that I can picture her so perfectly: little Elara, crouched among headstones, making a home out of the very stillness mortals fear, moving through death like it's a room she belongs in—my domain, my purpose.

The fact that she fits there, that she fits *with me*, twinges at that tightness in my chest. It's...unnerving.

"Suppose now that she's queen somehow...she has to take a husband." Mother shakes her head. "The girl can no longer hide in graves now, cozying up with death."

A chuckle slips out, only to die on the sharp memory of Elara grinding against me in that fresh soil, feigning a desire this traitorous body was all too eager to answer. Why would she ask to see my true form? Strategy? True curiosity?

Certainly not attraction. Her panting would've curdled to screams had I revealed myself. Even if her lust was real, it wouldn't survive the sight of a half-corpse god. A *monster.*

I give Mother a nod, if only to rip myself out of my mental ramblings. "She does seem to have a penchant for the morbid and the macabre."

Mother simply shrugs as she glances at the chapel doors. "She's...late."

"She's alive," I murmur. "That's enough punctuality for this kingdom."

Mother's lips thin at the bluntness, but she doesn't argue. Instead, she takes one more step closer and lowers her voice.

"I don't know where you came from," she says, "or how my daughter wound up wearing that mean-looking crown." Her eyes flick to the door again. "But if you're going to be her husband...be kind."

The request is so earnest it almost irritates me. "I do not believe myself to be particularly kind."

Mother nods slowly, as if she expected that, too. "Then at least be useful."

My teeth grind, an instinctive bristle I have to swallow before it shows. The absurdity of this is laughable—Death taking orders from his future mother-in-law. Yet the words sink in with a strange, grating weight, like a hook catching on something I forgot was there.

Just this damn cord.

I stare down at it again, yanking at it with two fingers, buying myself a deeper breath that smooths the ripples of my frustration. Despite the fact that Death can't die, I have no intention of letting a blade bleed my throat. Neither will

I indulge Elara's pathetic attempts at seduction, only further fanning her lunacy. No, I will simply...wait.

What are twenty years to me? Thirty?

A blink. A breath.

I'll remain true to my word and endure the tedium of her aging, of course. Watch the gray overtake the brown in her hair. Listen to her heart stutter to its inevitable—

"Get away from her!" The command cracks through the chapel.

I look up.

Elara stands in the archway of the heavy oak doors, caressed by deep green silk and velvet that make even the dim chapel light look rich. The bodice fits tightly around her shapely body before flaring out in heavy, embroidered folds. Long sleeves adorned with golden threads flutter behind her as she comes down the aisle in long strides that straighten her spine, lending her neck a posture of elegance.

It should delight me. It should amuse me, a dozen taunts lining my teeth like knives. Oh, look at how she finally abandoned her coarse deathcloth. Look how even a vulture can pass for a peacock if draped in prettier feathers.

My mouth parts, and out comes...

...nothing.

Because I'm fucking gaping, not at her gown, but at her hair: pinned up in the most straightforward, most practical twist, a few ornery strands refusing captivity at her temples. No jewels. No elaborate braids.

Just Elara, plain and simple.

Like death.

I ought to sneer. The fact that I can't seems far more damning than any vow I'm about to speak.

"Don't talk to her." Elara gently catches Mother's elbow

and draws her away from me, seating her on a nearby pew as she looks over her shoulder back at me. "You stay away from my family. You understand?"

I'm accustomed to being unwelcome among a mortal's loved ones, but the raw loathing etched into Elara's features somehow has my muscles tense. She looks at me with pure hatred.

Which should content me.

The sooner Elara realizes that she can't possibly love the god who lied, manipulated, and deceived her toward her slaughter, the faster she'll give up this ridiculous notion of breaking the curse.

And yet, looking into eyes that find me so thoroughly detestable... I find no joy in being proven right.

I simply raise a brow despite the sensation, shifting on the stone to banish the tension from my muscles. "Charming as always."

"Your Majesty," the priest says softly from the altar. "The ceremony..."

Elara turns from her mother and approaches the altar with the same sure stride she uses when she's walking into a house full of rot. She stops beside me, close enough that the heat of her body bleeds through silk and into the air between us.

"If you ever get near my family again," she grinds out, "I'll slit your throat for the sake of practice."

I make a point of not looking at her, and how difficult she renders even that. "Careful. Trust I carry my own frustrations...best not make me indulge you in them."

The priest clears his throat. "Join hands."

Elara extends her hand, mumbling under her breath, "Is that a threat?"

I take her palm, calloused from years of digging graves,

yet vibrating with life. "There are a great many ways a husband can deliver pain to his unruly wife. Involving my lap. And my hand. On your ass."

Her brow furrows, her mouth parting, then snapping shut when the meaning lands—red creeping up her throat in a furious flush.

She came to the tower a virgin, fumbling through the act with grit rather than grace. And I...I met her with nothing but eons of observation. And yet no amount of watching prepared me for the intensity of it, the over-whelming pleasure of being inside her. Of coupling like mortals do, of being so heatedly close with someone where I've only ever known cold solitude.

And that...that has sparked a hunger that is entirely, utterly inconvenient.

Elara's grip tightens around my hand, chin lifting in that annoying, stupidly alluring defiance of hers. "Can we get on with this?"

The priest flinches into action. "W-we are gathered here today," he squeaks, his eyes darting between us, "to join this man and this woman in the godly bonds of matrimony."

A scoff rumbles under my breath. "The only godly thing here is I."

"And yet you look like you're being dragged to your own hanging," Elara grates out of the corner of her mouth.

I keep my face smooth. "A hanging would have been preferable."

The priest looks back and forth between our bickering, sweat beading on his upper lip. "If we could... The binding?"

Miss Hampshire steps up with the grim efficiency of an executioner, her gaze fixed on the trailing ends of the cincture already constricting my chest. She doesn't hesitate. She seizes the cords dangling from my side and yanks them forward, wrapping them sharply around Elara's torso. She loops them once, twice, pulling the knot tight with a sudden, violent jerk that forces the breath from Elara's lungs. And mine.

That tension beneath my sternum blooms hot and brutal, sharp enough now to quicken my pulse as my gaze snaps to her. "I'm going to make you regret every second of this."

"Most husbands claim that's a wife's job." Elara trundles up the corners of her mouth, with struggle and effort, yes, but it is no less unnerving a sight. "There are many seconds in twenty years. More so in thirty."

I lower my voice to match her insolence. "Unless you have the decency to take off that crown before you tragically, but conveniently, fall off a horse next week."

"The rings," the priest says, voice thin.

A small velvet cushion is produced, bearing two plain bands. Gold, unadorned. Elara takes mine first and shoves it onto my finger with more force than ceremony, as if she means to bruise the vow into place. Then she holds out her hand without looking at me.

I take the ring and slide it onto her finger the way mortals do. And for a moment, I could swear I sensed my heartstring chime in her crown...

"Do you, Elara," the priest starts, voice strained, "take—"

"I do." Her answer is a bark as her fingers dig into mine. "I'll make it a point to sleep and bathe with the crown."

The priest blinks, flustered. "Your...Your Majesty—"

"I said yes." She shifts, letting the rope bite deeper, clench harder. "Get on with it."

"Do you, Vale," he continues, "take this woman as your wife, to have and to hold, to lead and to love?"

Something crawls low in my gut, letting my gaze shift to the mosaics set into the wall. Tiny tile kings and queens, forever frozen mid-vow, chests tied, their hearts full of love.

My ribs seem to curl inward.

Mortals are obsessed with it. Love.

It's a sickness of the mind. A voluntary lunacy. They chase it, sing of it, long for it—a deluded sentiment they crave as if it could ever end in anything other than pain. To love is to open your heart to the blade of grief, offering it a bloody sheath to land in before it cracks under the agony of loss.

Love is madness.

But it is a madness that cannot befall me. So what's the weight of this vow? Air, nothing more. Irrelevant and—

Hot breath shatters my thoughts, searing against the shell of my ear with how Elara has leaned in, her lips dangerously close as she whispers, "Tick-tock. Remember? You have places to be."

I fix my gaze on the priest with nothing short of a growl. "I do."

The priest swallows hard, but there's a sound of relief in the gulp. "In the sight of God, I pronounce you man and wife, 'til death do you part."

The words leave his mouth, letting ancient law amplify that tightness in my chest to a degree that makes me want to scream. Of all the absurdities I've observed over the centuries, my wife turning the rite around on me to break this curse is perhaps the most infuriating one.

Oh, how right she is.

How wrong she is...

SEVEN

Elara

"Bring me everything you can find," I say as I pace the length of my oaken desk in the royal chamber, candlelight flickering across the littering of books. "Every scrap of paper. Whatever Kael stacked, studied, or scribbled—I need to see it."

Miss Hampshire tosses a final piece of wood into the flames of the hearth, rises, and wipes her sooty nubs on her apron. "His Late Majesty wasn't fond of leaving ink behind."

I press a palm to my lower belly—something shifts there, deep and dull. "There has to be something."

Her gaze flicks toward the doors, then back to me. "He had to make certain Death never caught the scent of his plan. What he did put to paper, he hid like contraband. Burned the moment it served its purpose and—"

The doors burst open.

A young, breathless messenger stumbles in, followed by a minister I vaguely recall from a dizzying onslaught of introductions. His soft hands, which have likely never seen a day of hard labor, clutch a rolled map.

"Your Majesty! Forgive the intrusion, but the dam has failed!" the minister wails, practically shaking out the map over the books I carefully gathered from Kael's old room. "The Crying Valley is... It's gone."

"Gone, Your Majesty," the messenger heaves. "Saw it with my own eyes."

"The lowlands are underwater," the minister continues, sweat starting to shine on his bald head, flattening the few white wisps he has left. "Graves washed out. Coffins shattered. Corpses sick with rot are floating onto fields, into creeks." Panic flutters in his throat. "The risk of the pestilence spreading is immense, with the runoff chasing straight toward two other townships. What will you have us do?"

All moisture seems to evaporate from my mouth, leaving my tongue dry, my throat itchy. What will I have them do? I don't even know where these lowlands are. Never heard of them in my life!

"I—" My voice cracks.

I swallow. Swallow again, pulse fluttering against my throbbing esophagus. I know how to stretch a sack of flour.

Know how to lime a grave. But I have no fucking clue how to stop a damn flood.

Air whirls behind me with how Miss Hampshire busies herself with lighting another candle, only for her to shift closer to my back. "Have them open the dikes to the east." Her whisper barely reaches my ear, let alone the room. "It'll flood the grazing lands, but push the flood west and save the townships."

I glance over my shoulder, her eyes hard, unblinking beads. She's feeding me the words.

Turning back to the minister, I straighten my spine. "Open the eastern dikes."

The minister frowns. "Your Majesty, the grazing lands—"

"Won't feed a single gaping mouth if they're already stuffed with grave dirt," I say. "We'll deal with the consequences of the flooded grazing lands once they come into existence."

He blinks in surprise, offering no more pushback on the matter. "And...the bodies, Your Majesty?"

Moisture returns to my mouth, if only some. Graves. Corpses. That, I know!

"Where do most of them collect? Show me." When he points out the affected area on the map, I search its surroundings, gaze trailing over forest, rivers, mountains... Mountains. My nail runs along the words scribbled under the illustration of a triangle. "With how scarce the salt is, I assume this mine isn't currently being worked?"

"No, Your Majesty. Not in many years. It is nearly depleted."

"Perfect. Use harvest wagons with wide wheels to collect the bodies," I say. "Dump them into the mine. The salt will dry the bodies, contain the rot some."

"But the rites—"

"The dead care less about the rites than the living care about keeping rot away. Do it. Now."

The decisive crack of my order snaps them into motion. They bow, low and hurried, and scramble out the door.

When the latch clicks shut and silence returns, so does that dull twist in my lower belly. I press my palm against it once more, but it does nothing to stop how it radiates into my lower back.

"Your Majesty?" Miss Hampshire takes a step forward, eyeing my hand on my stomach.

"I'm fine," I say, straightening my spine. "Just...the corset thing."

"One of the crueler mandates of royal fashion, but it helps keep the chapel gossip down about the realm having a queen." She steps behind me once more. A tug here, a tug there, and the damn pressure eases its bite. "Better?"

"Yes, thank you." Nodding, I stride over to the window. "Also, thank you for helping me just now."

I pass the bloodstain that clings to the wooden floor. Whatever lay hidden beneath wool for decades has faded into a pale rust color ever since I ordered to have the rug removed. To show the handprint that sits deep inside the oak, raw and vulnerable—a daily reminder of what this curse took.

The things it can still take...

I close my eyes and press my forehead against the cool pane of the window. *Wed him. Bed him. Crown him dead and slit his throat.* How can something that sounds so neat be so impossible to achieve?

A throb starts behind my temple. Somehow, I managed to drag Death into a chapel and make him my husband, no matter how his vows dripped with pure poison. But the rest?

The memory of the open grave crashes over me, hot and humiliating. I tried to seduce him in the dirt, desperate and clumsy, and he shattered me without even undressing. He took my frantic offering and twisted it until I was the one unraveling, leaving me soaked in his seed but certainly not *bedded*.

How am I supposed to tempt a creature who knows desire as a weakness to be exploited? And why is he so adamant about clinging to this wretched curse? What does it give him, other than an endless harvest of souls he's tired of? He looks at the world like a man exhausted by his own doing, yet he fights to keep the very thing that seems to be draining him alive. Why?

"The original documents about the curse." I lift my head and look back to where Miss Hampshire draws the velvet comforter from my bed. "Where can I find it?"

I need to see it for myself. Maybe there's something Kael missed, a nuance hidden to male logic, a hint. And even if there isn't, being thorough, leaving nothing to chance will, at the very least, ease my mind some.

Miss Hampshire's gaze flicks to my crown, then away again, as if she doesn't like looking at the gold fused to my skull. "You may wish to try the—"

Three knocks on the door. Urgent.

An annoyed huff escapes me before I shout, "Enter!"

Hinges grind.

A young footman stumbles in, flushed and panting, mud on his shoes. He skids to a stop at the sight of me. "Your Majesty," he blurts, bowing too low, too fast. "There are people at the gates."

Miss Hampshire's eyes narrow. "How many?"

"Dozens. More and more each hour," he says, voice trembling. "Said they're not leaving until Her Majesty hears them out. Guards are getting nervous. One of them sent me."

Nerves tingle beneath my fingernails. "I'll receive them in the throne room, I guess, and listen to them. Every single one."

Miss Hampshire's gaze flicks to me. "You cannot hear all of them."

Desperation makes people unpredictable, and that's the last thing I need right now. "Things will get worse if I don't."

She mumbles something under her breath, but eventually, she gives a nod. "If I may suggest..." she says slowly. "Standing in a throne room is well and good, Your Majesty, but the people may find new hope if they see you out there. Especially with your...your husband."

"My husband?"

"At one of the orphanages perhaps." She pauses, her eyes flashing with a distinct, calculating intelligence. "If the Queen is seen walking the halls of the parentless, offering aid alongside her husband, it shows stability."

She's got a good point there. "I'll bring it up with the minister." And then I'll somehow have to convince Vale to do me this husbandly courtesy, which will undoubtedly be a whole new ordeal. "I'll still see these people, though. Is until the morning enough time to arrange this?"

"A prayer dressed up as a plan." Miss Hampshire crosses herself, then looks at the footman. "I will seek out the acting palace commander to make arrangements. Now go. Tell the guards to keep them still until the morn. Tell the kitchens to prepare a large kettle of runny porridge."

"Yes, Miss Hampshire," the footman says before he spins around to hurry out of the room.

The door shuts. My shoulders sag before I can stop them. The corset may be loosened, but the pressure in my skull remains—crown humming, bloodstain staring.

I drag a breath deep enough to hurt and let it out slowly. "I don't know how to do any of this," I admit, the words tasting like weakness and honesty all at once. "Floods. People at the gates, begging me for answers. And the worst part?" I scoff. "Even if I break this curse and stop the rot, I'll still be stuck being queen."

Miss Hampshire watches me, the tired lines around her mouth deepening, her half-hand tapping once against her apron, like she's counting the beats it takes for a woman to crack. "Time never made for a poor teacher." A pause, then her gaze hardens back into competence. "The chapel."

My mind stutters, trying to catch up. "What?"

"The documents of the deal struck between the crown's first king and Death," she says. "Might be in the olden language, but the chapel is where you should find it, Your Majesty."

My fingers mindlessly stroke over my belly. "Right. I'll talk to a priest after I listen to the people."

Miss Hampshire's eyes narrow on me. She steps closer, her tone dropping into something that sounds almost maternal. "The monthly bleed coming?"

I frown. That's something I haven't even considered, making me hesitate for a moment before I say, "I don't know. It's been forever since the last time."

Miss Hampshire nods. "A pillow of warmed chestnuts then, just in case," she says briskly. "I will have a maid fetch it for you."

"Thank you."

She leaves, and the room exhales. I don't ready myself for bed. I don't even sit. I can't.

I return my attention to the window, the energy inside me a mix of nervous caution and excited anticipation. One step closer to breaking this curse, but it seems like merely a hand in a furlong. How am I supposed to love a creature as vicious and heartless as Death?

"It is impossible," I whisper to the glass, the condensation from my breath fogging the view of the outside world.

The air in the room shifts.

It isn't a sound. It's a pressure change, like the sudden drop in the atmosphere before lightning strikes. The hair on my arms stand up, faster when the shadows in a corner don't just lengthen, but detach.

They stitch themselves together into black cloth. It ripples through the air before it settles into velvet and black curls, darkness weaving rapidly into the shape of Vale.

"Wife," he purrs, and the word is not affectionate. "You have gates full of mourners. Floodwater full of corpses. A brother drowning in rot." A lopsided smirk lets his teeth flash. "Tell me...do you love me yet?"

EIGHT

Elara

Tell me...do you love me yet?

Heat floods my veins with such speed, my entire body itches when my eyes lock with the green of his. "We both know you're making that quite difficult."

Crossing his arms behind his back, Vale strides out of the shadows, only for his boots to stop where the moon floods the floor. "Oh?"

"Women warned me that husbands get irritating after a

while, you know," I say. "Then mine shows up, annoying me without even a grace period."

Amusement curls his lips into a lopsided smirk. "Presume there's always the option of divorce. Some kings have granted a handful in the past. I guess so could a..." His gaze trails over my black corset and down the equally dark silken train. "...a queen."

"Is that a request?" The smile I work onto my lips is about as sweet as he is annoying. "Denied."

A muscle jumps in his jaw—a telltale sign of how hard he tries to maintain his smirk—eyes drifting to the silver border on the floor that shines the tip of his boot. The moon is high tonight, full enough to bathe the room.

Full enough to make *him* cautious.

"Why don't you come here to look at the moon with me?" I ask softly, if only to mock him. "It's illuminating the statue of you in the gardens."

"I have seen the moon." A bored kind of exhale. "I have seen it wax and wane for eons. It doesn't impress me. Close the drapes, *wife*."

The command carries more than mere annoyance. It has weight—habitual, practiced, like a man slamming a door before anyone can glimpse what's behind it. Why?

My mind flicks through scraps of memories. *"I dislike the way light invents me when I'm not paying attention,"* he once said in that carriage. *"Power does not quicken every pulse the way songs promise,"* he'd sneered. As if he'd learned long ago that his true form is too appalling to be seen, too horrendous to be desired.

Too disgusting to be loved?

Something shifts inside my core at that thought...

"Why, *husband?*" A tilt of my head. "Are your bones shy?"

He exhales a long, controlled breath—like he's forcing himself to rein in his temper already, mere seconds into this conversation. "I asked you to close the drapes."

I turn around fully, leaning back against the sill. "And I'm asking for the second time now to let me see you. The real you."

"In twenty to thirty years."

The longer he stands there, unmoving, the clearer all this becomes. He isn't protecting me from the sight of him; he's protecting himself from my reaction. The flinch. The scream.

The rejection.

But what would happen if I didn't flinch? What would happen if I traced the clean curve of exposed ribs with curiosity? Ran my palm over the pale plains of muscle held together by tendons with fascination? Would he recoil?

Or would he melt into the accepting touch?

As if he read my thoughts, his smirk turns into a sneer. "You are tedious."

"And you're vain."

He straightens, the barb landing exactly where I aimed it. For a heartbeat longer, we just stare at each other—him, an arrogant god refusing to concede an inch, and me, a simple gravedigger refusing to back down. But the stalemate gets boring after a minute, and I have a curse to break.

"Fine!" I huff, rolling my eyes with exaggerated surrender. I reach behind me, snatching the heavy velvet and yanking it across the glass. The room plunges into candle-streaked darkness, the silver light choking off to the distinctive, confident click of his boots on the wood.

Just as he looms into range, I grab the fabric again and whip it back—not all the way. Just a sliver. Just a gap. Just a bright, sharp blade of moonlight carving skin and meat off his bony finger.

The way he curls the digit into his meaty palm with arthritic clicks rips a strange sound from my lungs.

It's a laugh, low and throaty enough that Vale narrows his eyes at me with exactly the anger I expected. But there's something else swirling in the golden specks of his irises. Confusion. Perhaps even a flustering.

Until he shakes his head, as if physically dislodging his shock, and sidesteps the beam of light with predatory grace. Before I can twitch, his hand clamps around my wrist, letting the velvet drapes fall shut with a heavy *swoosh* that plunges us back into orange shadow.

"Glad to be of amusement," he grinds out, the words vibrating against my skin as he uses the momentum to spin me, slamming my back against the wall beside the window. "Married for less than two days, and already, I'm starting to understand why husbands avoid their wives and seek the company of whores instead."

"Spoken like a man who is oh-so fond of lies and deceptions," I snarl. "Truths aren't nearly as comfortable, which wives don't bother to serve anything but cold."

"Truth?" In one smooth motion, he pins my captured wrist high above my head, his body pressing into mine, heavy and hot and overwhelmingly close, trapping me between the cool plaster and the solid, angry warmth of him. "The truth, little wife, is that you're no closer to breaking the curse. You think shackling me with this marriage was a victory?" He leans in, the green fire in his eyes burning with ancient, bitter amusement. "You've merely shackled yourself to a corpse that even the ground refuses to swallow. This plan of Kael's that you're trying to bring to fruition is questionable at best."

"Oh, trust me, I did question it plenty," I spit back, refusing to shrink away from the volatility of his stupid temper. "It did cross my mind that seduction was a doomed strategy for something that apparently never touched a woman before. Who was to say you even had a taste for women?" I tilt my head, voice dropping to a conspiratorial whisper. "Perhaps you'd prefer a *husband*."

He doesn't blink, doesn't bristle. The taunt slides off him like water off oiled silk, his expression one of bored indulgence.

"But then," I continue, keeping my voice light, casual, "I remembered the tower. You pushed inside me and spilled within five strokes. And in the grave? It didn't take much more than that, did it?" I click my tongue sympathetically. "Death *is* a lover...just a poor one."

His pupils dilate, swallowing the irises, and his grip on my wrist tightens just enough to sting. The boredom vanishes—if only for a second—before he wrenches his features back into a mask of aloof cruelty.

"My wife sounds frustrated tonight," he murmurs, his tone sliding into a dangerous purr. "Is she angry because she's growing desperate? Or because I stood up and left her in the dirt, covered in my seed but utterly unsatisfied?"

He doesn't wait for my retort.

His free hand slides down my flank, grabbing fistfuls of silk, bunching the fabric upward until the air of the room hits the heated skin of my thighs. There's no fumble, no hesitation. He knows exactly where to go. His long fingers hook the thin fabric of my undergarments, brutally shoving them aside before his thumb strokes over the sensitive pearl at my center.

A ragged gasp tears from my throat. My head falls back

against the wall, my hips bucking instinctively into his palm. "Oh my god."

"Uh-huh." He leans in, his breath tingling the lobe of my ear while his thumb circles the nub—once, twice, a maddeningly precise friction. "Do you love me yet, Elara?"

"Bastard…" The word dissolves into a whimper, but I refuse to surrender the offensive.

My hand snakes down between our bodies, seeking the strain in his breeches. As expected, he's granite beneath the leather, a furious contradiction to the poison he spits. I cup him, squeezing his thick cock, and his breath instantly turns jagged.

He retaliates, his thumb working faster, harder, trying to drive me over the edge before I can unravel him. "You best stop, Elara. Or I might have to tell you how badly I want you to trip and break your neck."

"Careful. The more you try to convince me you're heartless, the more I wonder what exactly you're guarding so fiercely." I struggle against the stiff waistband, forcing my fingers past the fabric until I hit searing heat. "A man who truly has no heart"—I wrap my hand around the bare velvet of him, swirling my thumb over the weeping head—"wouldn't need to shout about it quite so loudly."

He groans, a rough, guttural sound that vibrates against my lips. His forehead drops to my shoulder, his control shattering, but his voice is a jagged whisper in my ear. "Then best remember what happens to unruly wives."

"I've seen women sport bruises like jewels." I don't halt the rhythm of my hand against his slick skin. Neither does he, spreading two fingers to trap my clit between them as he strokes back and forth. "I've watched neighbors spit teeth onto the floorboards after a husband's chaotic rage, only to crawl back to them before the blood even dries. I've seen them cling to the legs of the men who broke them, confessing love."

"That's not true love, but—mmm." His thick length surges in my hand, stretching to an aching hardness and twitching against my palm with a need that utterly betrays his composure. "Come to think...*not true love* might serve me even better than your hate."

He yanks me from the wall by my wrist. With a force that leaves no room for resistance, he spins me around and bends me over the heavy oak desk. Sharp spines of books dig through the map and into my ribs as he flattens a large hand between my shoulder blades, pinning me inextricably to the wood. With his free hand, he bunches my skirts, dragging the heavy material up my legs until it piles at my waist, leaving me shivering and exposed.

My boldness falters, a tremor of genuine unease threading through the question. "W-what are you doing?"

He doesn't answer.

For a tormenting moment, there's only the sound of his ragged breathing behind me. His fingertip ghosts over my entrance, tracing the rim in a slow, maddening circle as if—

The touch vanishes.

The air hangs suspended.

Slap.

A sharp blow hits my ass, so violent it jars the breath right out of my lungs. My mind staggers behind the sensation, failing to process the spanking until the pain blooms —a searing, white-hot heat that scorches the surface of my skin before sinking heavy and cruel into the flesh, the shock of it vibrating down to the bone.

"Do you love me yet?" The question hangs in the air, mocking and sharp, before his hand descends again.

The sound is as jarring as the sting, a whip-like report

that echoes off the ceiling. I grit my teeth, burying my face into the crook of my arm to stifle the cry clawing at my throat, but he offers me no reprieve. He strikes again, harder, the blow landing perfectly over the ghost of the last.

"How is divorce sounding now?" he growls, his voice a low rumble in the room. "Still denied?"

I whimper against the hairs that rise along my arm. "You asshole!"

His next strike is quieter. Not due to lack of precision, lighting a fire across my skin that burns its way between my legs, but because he chuckles.

"Is this the love you spoke of, Elara? Hmm?" His next slap is duller somehow, mutating into a throbbing heat that spreads low in my belly, letting a current of energy tingle around my clit. "Can you feel it yet?"

My mind spins, fading the cruelty of his strikes. The dominance of his heavy hand holding me down no longer feels caging. It feels...steadying.

A shameful, liquid warmth unfurls between my thighs. My muscles ease, no longer bracing against the next impact. When his hand lands again, my hips don't jerk away in recoil; they buck backward, a subtle, involuntary seek for the friction.

That's when the rhythm breaks.

Vale stops.

He hovers there behind me, breathing hard, the violence in the room suddenly suspended in a thick, confusing silence.

Why did he stop?

Slowly, his hand slides from the burning curve of my ass, down, down, until his fingers curl beneath me. He brushes against my folds, seeking the entrance, and slips effortlessly into a slick, drenched heat.

I shudder, my forehead resting against the desk, unable to hide the evidence of my body's strange reaction. He drags two fingers through the heavy cream, coating them, noisily testing the viscosity of my desire with a smack of his tongue.

"Interesting..." His voice is thin, breathless. "I cannot tell if I struck too hard...or not hard enough."

With a rough growl, he slides his fingers inside me again, letting a beckoning motion scrape against my inside. My knees buckle, knocking against the wood, but his other hand presses down harder, keeping me bent, keeping me steady.

"You are impossible, Elara," he snarls as he drives his fingers in a rhythm that is urgent, angry. "Frustrating, maddening woman. You're so damn stubborn that you refuse to indulge me even with your pain."

The pleasure is immediate and blinding, fueled by the adrenaline of his violence. I gasp, my head tilting to its side, chasing the friction. I'm close, so shamefully close, my body winding tight, a sob gathering in my throat—

His fingers vanish.

Crack.

His palm strikes my raw skin. Not hard enough to injure, but sharp enough to shock the pleasure right out of my body. The climax dissolves into a frustrated ache.

He *tsks*. "Don't you dare."

Vale immediately resumes the assault, harder this time, his thumb grinding down on my clit while his fingers plunder the wet heat inside. He's relentless, stealing my breath, forcing the sensation back up the mountain at a breakneck pace.

"You cling to the things that should repel you," he

mutters, his breaths coming faster. "You should be running away, Elara. *Why aren't you running?*"

I can't answer. I can only keen as the pressure builds again, higher, hotter, a wave crashing over my head until—

The next blow lands on the other cheek, stinging and rude. The orgasm shatters again, leaving me trembling and whining, frustrated tears pricking my eyes.

"Please," I beg.

"Please, what?" His tone is a taunt. "Please stop? Please hurt you more?" Before I can answer, he growls, "Be still."

The command is guttural, making me freeze before I feel the pulsing, searing warmth of his crown press against my drenched entrance. "Vale, please…"

But he doesn't push inside.

Instead, he drags the weeping, velvet head of his cock through my slick folds, coating himself in the mess I made. He groans, a low vibration that rattles through the oak, hips jerking slightly as if it takes every ounce of his ancient willpower not to bury himself to the hilt inside me.

"You want this, don't you?" he whispers, sliding the broad head up and down, lubricating the path, teasing the entrance but refusing to enter. "Want me to push inside. To fuck you. To *bed* you." He pulls back an inch, denying me. "Bringing you one imaginary step closer to that deluded goal of yours."

I mewl in frustration, my hands scrabbling against the parchment on the desk. "Please make me finish."

"I can't. I'm a poor lover, remember?"

He presses the head of his cock directly against my swollen, tormented clit and begins to grind there. Intense, rhythmic slides, the ridge of his length gliding over my nerve endings, over and over, while the air fills with the sounds of his own unraveling.

"Fuck," he hisses through clenched teeth, every thrust of his hips punctuated by a guttural groan.

He wants inside. I can feel the desperate, jerking seek of his body. I can feel the way he bears down, as if he is about to shatter his own rule and impale me, only to violently drag himself back up to my clit at the last second. He's panting, ragged, harsh gasps tearing from his throat.

He's right there, teetering on the edge with me. I can feel his tremors shaking into mine, until he slams his groin against my ass one last time, ruthlessly grinding his hard shaft against my swollen bud in little pulsations.

The sensation is too much—too heavy, too direct. My world whites out. I scream, my body seizing in a violent release that ripples through every muscle.

And it shatters him.

With a roar that sounds like it was ripped from the chest of a beast, he stiffens behind me. I feel the hot, wet release as he spills over, his seed spurting in heavy, rhythmic jets that coat my curls, run to collect at my lower lips, only to pearl down the insides of my trembling thighs.

The heavy weight of his hand finally lifts from between my shoulder blades, leaving a cold phantom impression where his heat had grounded me. He steps back, adjusting his clothes with shaking hands, his chest still heaving as he looks down at the mess he made.

"Hopefully that improved your mood," he says, his voice raspy, stripped of its usual smooth cadence. "But I refuse to indulge your delusions."

I turn slowly, my knees trembling, and lean back against the edge of the desk for support. I should be frustrated, but I'm too thoroughly unraveled, my body feeling heavy and loose, buzzing with a satiation that borders on narcotic.

Besides…what is there to be frustrated about?

I look at him—hair disheveled, eyes dark and blown wide. My husband gave me something far more valuable than a simple bedding. He gave me a tell.

If there's one thing I've learned about Vale, it is that where he offers no resistance, there's no value. But where he fights?

There's the path.

I catch my breath and gift him a languid, knowing smile. "For an act you claim is inconsequential to the curse's undoing," I murmur, tilting my head, "you certainly try to avoid it desperately."

His hands slow on the fastenings of his breeches. The tension returns to his jaw, but he doesn't scowl. Instead, a slow, terrifyingly beautiful smile curves his lips.

"There is a…new element, *my love*. One I would rather avoid, lest we complicate things further." He reaches out and slides a finger deep inside once more. I gasp at the intrusion, sensitive and swollen, as he swipes through the slickness, only for him to withdraw. His eyes lock onto mine, darkening as he brings the finger up between us, the scent of coins filling the air. "You, Elara, are starting to bleed again."

Elara

The hearth in Daron's room burns low, settled to glowing coals for the night. A quilt lies over my brother's body, hiding the marbling that's spread from his shoulders over toward his collarbone. His chest rises and falls with less violence today.

Still wet. Still wrong.

But not as frantic as yesterday.

I try not to let that small mercy fool me into believing the rot has grown kind and shift on my chair, turning my attention back to the table. Documents are spread across the little table by the window, delivered carefully by Miss Hampshire earlier tonight: parchment more ancient than the oldest grave back home, edges brittle and yellowed, ink faded to ghost-gray strokes.

Father of Nothing, some priest called Death in one of the documents buried somewhere at the bottom. My fingers drift absently to my lower belly, to the lingering ache there now that my bleeding is finally easing after a few days.

Can Death even father a child?

He seems to think so, which indeed is a worrisome thought at best. If I fall pregnant with his child, would it be godly? Mortal? And how would it change—

Now I'm getting ahead of myself.

I chuckle into the room as if my situation is funny, then groan until the candle beside me flickers because it's anything but. For all I know, his caution is just a convenient excuse to avoid bedding, a lie to distract me from a goal he's making impossible to reach.

A polite rap on the door, followed by the bristle of Miss Hampshire's skirts as she enters with a basket clasped underarm. "The straw you requested, Your Majesty."

"Put it beside the bed," I say with a jut toward the blood-drowned bucket that already rests there. "I'll take care of it myself in a bit."

She does as told before she straightens and looks at the littered table, eyes narrowing. "Your Majesty might wear a crown now, but even queens need rest. Would you like me to have a maid prepare your bed?"

"Not yet." My fingers lift to my face, rubbing the itch from my eyes. "How do I get my husband to show me his full true form?"

My head of staff gives a high-pitched, almost offended

huh. "Whyever would you want to see such a gruesome thing?"

"I have a feeling it matters." I press my thumb to the edge of a brittle page, grounding myself in its roughness. Vale fights the bedding tooth and claw, but what if I've been aiming at the wrong target all along? Maybe I'm not supposed to seduce Vale...but Death. "If only I could fool him again, maybe he'd owe me another wish." My gaze drops to the line of ink. "I could demand he show me his bones. Or better yet, ask for a proper bedding."

Miss Hampshire's brows lift, straining the angry-red wound where her pustule finally popped a few days ago. Then she turns to shake at a curtain. And another, her eyes narrowing as if palacekeeping is fueling her thoughts.

"Your first wish was only granted because you convinced him you had plotted behind his back with the late king, may God rest his poor soul." Her half-hand taps her apron when she turns back around to face me. Her gaze meets mine, sharp, calculating. "It sounds to me as if you have fooled him a second time already."

"Technically, he fooled himself." And yet, her words settle into me like a spark finding dry kindling, small but viciously bright.

"One must wonder if technicalities matter." Miss Hampshire curtsies—stiff, habitual—then slips out, leaving the room to hush and candlelight.

A second wish. A second lever.

For a moment, that spark flares...only to be blown out by one drafty fact. Demanding payment requires me to confess that my first wish never had a foundation to begin with. And that's a risk that might not just crumble my marriage into a divorce, but straight up annulment.

A husband unmade. A god released, making me lose the

only chain I've managed to get around his throat thus far. And then what?

The sense of defeat is a deadweight that pulls my chin toward my chest, but I stop it by anchoring my gaze to a document before me. The script is nothing like I've ever seen. The letters don't flow. They snarl: sharp angles, strange loops, marks above vowels like little teeth.

A part of the curse in the olden language.

My gaze slides to its original translation on the right...

> *"To break the Crown, love must rise,*
> *The sovereign binding Death*
> *in lover's guise.*
> *In the bed of the night,*
> *the sovereign shall yield,*
> *Receiving Death on the corpse's field.*
> *For the string restores*
> *not by the blade's cruel art,*
> *But snaps only within*
> *the shattered heart."*

A knock sounds at the door.

"Why don't they ever leave me alone?" A huff escapes me, pure annoyance scraping my throat. "Enter."

The door opens a cautious crack. The young priest who wed me slips in, face drawn tighter than that day. His eyes flick first to Daron—on the bed, pale and still—then to me and the papers spread across the desk.

His mouth tightens. "Your Majesty called for a priest?"

"Close the door."

He obeys, though his fingers linger on the latch as if he'd rather be elsewhere. "How can I assist, Your Majesty?"

I tap the parchment. "Translate."

His brows lift. "Your Majesty?"

"This." I slide the top sheet toward him. "The old tongue. I want you to read it to me in the common language."

He steps only as close as he needs to scan the scribbles. "Your Majesty, there already *is* a translation right beside it. It says it right there in the title. *The Stanza of Death's Heart.*"

"I'm aware. Read it about twenty times now, and I still want the original read to me as you translate."

"The crown's rites were translated centuries ago," he says carefully. "This particular document might only recently have re-emerged, but I assure you the translation was—"

"Ordered by men greedy enough to trade lives for power," I finish and flick the parchment. "I don't trust a single thing in this castle unless I see it with my own two eyes. And even then, I might still be suspicious of it." Another tap on the parchment, harder this time. "Read this to me."

The young man looks as if I've asked him to swallow a dagger. "This is not a simple—"

"Do not talk to me about simple." I sit back, forcing myself to breathe. "Just...read."

His gaze flicks to Daron, as if trying to remind himself there are more sacred things than monarchy. Then his eyes return to the parchment.

"Your Majesty, this language is dead." His voice is careful, almost reverent. "Even in the chapel, even among priests, it is no longer spoken. I...I cannot simply read this." He hesitates. "If you give me time, I shall provide you with a new, true translation," he says, only to add quickly, "Unadulterated."

Strength leaks out of my spine, making it curl against the backrest of the chair. "How long?"

"The language is dense, often...often metaphorical," he says, his voice rubbing itself thinner on each syllable. "Diacritics change not only pronunciation, but references in their entirety. To re-translate the entire... It requires cross-referencing with texts kept in the lower vaults to—"

"How. Long."

He swallows. "Days," he admits. "Perhaps a week. It depends on the condition of the reference material."

Days. A week.

Nausea churns my stomach, more violently when I look over at Daron. "Start tonight. If I find you sleeping, I hope it's in a position where you lean slumped over your lectern."

"Y-yes, Your Majesty." He quickly gathers the parchment and scrambles backward with several bows. "I will translate it as quickly as I can. *Faithfully.*"

He turns and practically runs, his robes billowing behind him. The door clicks shut, sealing the room once more in its suffocating quiet.

I let out a long, ragged exhale, pressing my fingers to my temples. I feel stretched thin, like rope frayed to the breaking point. The encounter with Vale—the violence, the pleasure, the strange, terrifying intimacy of it—still hums beneath my skin.

A distraction I can't afford.

And now this.

"I was beginning to worry," a rasping voice creaks from the shadows, "that the priest was here to measure me for the box."

My head snaps around.

Daron is watching me, his eyes much brighter, shockingly clear against the candlelight. But that's not what makes my lips part while something even brighter whirls through my core. No, it's that smug grin on his face.

"Daron." I cross the room in two strides, that twitching on the corners of my mouth something I can't—and don't want to—suppress as I drop to my knees beside the bed. "You idiot."

His smirk widens—crooked, boyish, infuriatingly alive for a face that should look like it's already halfway gone. "Still smart enough not to get myself stuck with a crown and a rotting kingdom."

"Oh, shut up," I breathe, and the sound that comes out is half laugh, half relief. I grab his hand again like it's an anchor. "You shouldn't be witty while you're pretending to be dying."

He squeezes my fingers, weak but deliberate. "Family curse, how we're all feeling right at home in the grave," he rasps. "Heard there's more than one curse going around here."

"What did you hear?"

"The lady without fingers mumbled something once." He inhales slowly, as if each word costs him breath he can barely spare. "That the crown...brings the rot. That you're trying to fix it."

My throat tightens, but I keep stroking the ridge of his knuckles. "It's complicated."

"And," he continues, eyes narrowing with a spark of mischief, "I heard you got married."

My molars grind. "Also complicated."

He lifts a brow, shaky but no less taunting. "Is he one of those noble peacocks? Is he handsome?"

I roll my eyes. "Don't start."

"Handsome," he decides. "That's new. You always said you'd marry a corpse."

That shuts me up for a second. "Did I?"

"Years ago." Daron laughs, small, wheezy, but real. His grin softens. "What's his name?"

My throat tightens again. I hate how saying it feels like inviting him further into something I want to keep him from.

"Vale."

Daron's eyes narrow, processing. "Vale," he repeats, then coughs softly. "That's a place, not a name."

That rips a chuckle from me, a reluctant spark of humor warming the tension from my throat. "How are you feeling?"

He shifts slightly, wincing. "Better."

The word lands like honey in a starving mouth, letting my hope leap before I can leash it. "Pain?"

He blinks, eyes drifting toward the ceiling. "Less pain," he says slowly. "Less itch. Less…" His throat works. "Less everything."

"Your ear? It's not itching anymore?"

Daron shakes his head. "No." He shifts, frowning slightly as his bones press against the mattress. "Help me sit up? If I have to look at that ceiling one more hour, I shall die of boredom before the sickness takes me."

Nodding, I rise to sit beside him. "Alright. Gently now."

I slide my arm behind his shoulders—his body light like a bundle of dry kindling—and hoist him up against the pillows. He gasps, his arms twitching uselessly before they settle once more.

"Better." He looks at me, his gaze scanning my face with a terrifying perception. "Do you remember when you asked if you looked royal?" His breath hitches, but he grins anyway. "You said you'd sell my hands to the king. Saints, Elara, now you *are* the king, and my hands have gotten pretty useless." Daron's mouth twitches, grin lifting even higher. "Can't even become your guard and fight off your enemies with a stale crust."

A soft laugh breathes past my lips as my vision starts to swim. "At least you haven't lost your wit. That's more than most guards have to begin with."

His grin fades into something softer, a quiet sort of nostalgia settling in the lines around his eyes. "You remind me of Father," he whispers. "Especially when you're blunt like that."

The mention of him is a sudden, sharp ache in the center of my chest. "I miss him."

"Me, too. Do you remember the harvest before the big freeze? The year I ate too many candied apples?"

I blink, the memory rising unbidden through the haze of my grief. "You threw up on the walk home."

"Before that," he corrects. "I got tired. My legs were too short to keep up with the crowds. Father didn't say a word. He just lifted me up and put me on his shoulders." He presses his eyes shut is if to enhance the memory. "I remember the smell of his coat: pipe tobacco and wet felt. I fell asleep up there, high above everyone else. I felt...invincible. Like nothing in the world could touch me as long as I was held by him."

A tear slips free, tracking down my cheek. "I hate that the grief is the only thing I have left of him."

Daron's thumb brushes against my knuckles. The touch is weak, but his eyes, when they open again, are lucid and burning with a sudden, fierce intensity.

"No," he says, his voice finding a surprising strength. "You've got it backward, big sister. Grief is just love hiding in a mourning dress, piling up inside you because the person you want to give it to isn't there to take it."

I sniff, wiping my face on my sleeve, abandoning a queenly dignity I never had to begin with. "Doesn't make it hurt less."

"Pain is a good thing." He lets out a dry, rattling breath that sounds painfully like a chuckle. "Reminds us that we're alive, right?"

The words land gently, yet they burn somehow. I'm not sure if a boy whose voice hasn't even fully dropped should make peace with agony as a companion in this way.

I stroke an oily strand from his face. "Well, no box for you just yet."

His boyish grin curls up once more, wobbling at the corners with the strain before he murmurs, "Not yet."

Elara

The woods behind the palace don't like visitors.

They keep their paths narrow and their branches low, as if daring you to stumble over the half-crumbled headstone of the odd grave here and there. Somewhere far off, an owl hoots toward the moon, then goes quiet, like it regrets announcing itself.

Good.

Quiet is what I need.

Stillness, too, though I've learned over the last two days that Death listens to my summons with the same enthusiasm as a mule listens to commands: whenever he feels like it.

I stop in a small clearing where the branches open just enough to let moonlight fall like a silver veil across a large fallen tree trunk. Presume my husband is busy with more pressing matters. Like collecting the souls of those dying from a pestilence that only exists because he has a strange fondness for this fucking curse.

Damp cold settles into my lungs with my next inhale. As does a woody undercurrent, slightly spiced with hints of apricot and nuts. I knew it!

Following the length of the rotten trunk, I scan the shadows for the black-dotted caps of ashmorels. To ease the trembling in her fingers, Mother had said before she wrinkled her nose at the kitchen's sparse selection of dried herbs, although—

"Whenever," comes from the shadows beside me, "has there been a story about a young woman going into the forest at night, during pestilence and famine, *alone*, and it ended well?"

I straighten my spine, then I turn to the darkness just as I tap my nail against my crown with a dull *clank*. "Temporarily undying, remember?"

"As am I, albeit more permanently so." Vale leans against the trunk of an ancient oak, its canopy of decaying leaves and gnarly branches shielding him well from the moon. "And yet I once took a fall in this form, a great many feet down a cliff, shattering too many bones to count, but that was only half as miserable as the driftwood that rose bloodied from my guts." Arms crossed in front of his vest, he lifts one leg, pressing the sole of his boot against the tree. "An experience I would wish on nobody. Least of all my dearest wife."

I give him my sweetest of smiles. "Pretty kind words coming from a man who was dead set on marching me to my execution mere weeks ago."

Vale's gaze drifts over me in that calculating way of his, only for him to sigh. "What are you doing out here?"

"Searching for mushrooms. Searching for my husband." I take a step toward him, mud slurping beneath my boots. "You're late."

His mouth curves, thin. "Late for what?"

"Supper," I say with a shrug. "Of all the hardworking husbands out there, I'd expect you to be the most eager to come home to rest your bones."

That curve straightens, banishing all bemusement from his features. "What do you want, Elara?"

"Who says I want anything?"

"Oh, please, do you truly believe I know my wife so little?" Vale pushes himself off the trunk. He takes one slow step forward, yet remains under the oak's dark shelter. "You only ever become this chatty when you think you've already won the argument," he says, his voice a low, dry rasp that makes the fine hairs on my arms stand up. "That treacherous little smile of yours? We both know it's a taunt. So, I'm asking again before I get bored and converse with the dead instead...what do you want?"

Whatever nerves are starting to drum against my esophagus, I swallow down. "I want to see you."

Vale's eyes flicker. "You see me."

"The real you." I inch closer, careful not to step into the tree's shadow, careful to keep the moon between us. "Show me Death."

Vale's gaze flicks to the bright clearing, then back to me, displeasure tightening his jaw. "We've had this conversation." He turns away, shadows seemingly melting into his black breeches. "I have no time for our marital disputes as if—"

"It's not a dispute!" I call behind him, pulse quickening in my wrists. "It's a demand for a wish."

His boot halts mid-lift, stalling there for a second before he spins back around, a black strand settling wild across his forehead with how his gaze tilts. "I beg your pardon?"

"Assuming that…" I say slowly, testing the words, the sharp edge of their risk, "that my first wish was based merely on your *assumption* of having been fooled…" My breath fogs into the cold. "…what would happen to the wish I made?"

Vale's eyes narrow. "Elaborate."

The word is clipped. Demanding.

I keep my face calm, even as my pulse begins to thunder. It's a gamble. A terrifying, irrevocable gamble. Sure, having fooled him by going along with his assumption buys me a wish, but what if admitting that I never plotted with Kael renders my marriage null and void?

My throat narrows.

Well, then I'll simply use the leverage of this second wish to demand our marriage remains intact. It won't get me any closer to breaking the curse, true, but I won't let myself lose my footing, either.

It is a lateral move at worst.

A checkmate at best.

I take a breath, letting the cold air brace me. "If I told you that I never plotted my coronation with Kael. If I told you that…that he ripped me from under the table that morning and simply shoved the knife into my hand with the plea to kill him, without me understanding why. Would that void my last wish? Our marriage?"

The silence of the woods is heavy for a long, terrifying moment. The air pressure drops, popping in my eardrums.

He exhales at the speed of a maggot crossing a grave. "So you're a liar, same as me?"

"I didn't lie." Not entirely. "You simply voiced what you wanted to hear, and I didn't correct you."

"Is that so?" he bites out. "And now you're here, testing whether you can wring another wish out of me?"

My muscles tense. "Answer my question."

Vale's mouth curves, sharp and bitter. "You want me to say no."

"I want you to tell me the truth."

His nostrils flare. The tendons in his neck strain against his collar, and I watch him grind his molars with enough force to crack stone. I brace myself, waiting for the fury, waiting for the whiplash of his temper.

But the eruption never comes.

Instead, he shuts his eyes tight, shaking his head slowly as if to himself. When his lashes lift again, the fire in his gaze isn't aiming to scorch me. It's burning inward.

He isn't furious that I fooled him.

He's furious that he fooled himself.

"I cannot undo what has been bound." His voice is sharper, resentment threaded through it. "The answer to your question, *wife*...is no."

A spark of new hope. So the marriage stands, securing me a second wish.

Vale watches my face and knows exactly what I'm thinking. "Oh," he murmurs. "For once, I seem to have made my wife *very* happy."

I lift my chin. "I wish—"

"I know exactly what you want to wish for," he purrs,

lifting his hand to beckon me toward him. "A bedding, isn't it?"

Heat crawls up my throat. Fear, too, once I walk toward him, if only to buy myself time to think. The bedding is essential, that much I'm certain of, but...is it more important than getting him to show me his true form?

My mind flashes to the stanza on the paper. *In the bed of the night, the sovereign shall yield, Receiving Death on the corpse's field.*

Not Vale.

Death.

On a corpse's field, which—a glance through the woods is all it takes for my eyes to snatch on the lower graveyard nearby—this should serve. I can wish for him to fuck me. I can wish for him to show his true form. I won't make myself look a fool by asking for both, inviting his cheery denial.

So which one?

I don't realize how close I am to the ancient oak until Vale's hand slides down my waist, palm flattening over my hip. His thumb strokes once, slowly, the touch more warning than caress.

"How would you like it? Against the tree? Right here in the dirt?" His whisper finds my neck—just breath and heat and the faint scrape of his lips hovering like a threat. "I don't recall the wording of the rites mentioning any details on *where* on your body you're supposed to receive me. Maybe I'll choose your ass and take my time for once."

That muscle clenches at the mere thought of that invasion. "You didn't even hear what I demand."

He scoffs, his other hand sliding down my thigh, fingers seeking the edge of my skirt. "What else could it possibly be?"

My breath catches when his fingers graze the inside of my thigh. "Maybe I want you to show me Death."

His hand freezes.

Very interesting...

For one suspended heartbeat, the woods seem to stop breathing. The playful, predatory heat of his body turns to stone against mine, the air curdling with a tension that has nothing to do with surprise and everything to do with fear.

Then, just as quickly, the rigidity shatters.

"Don't be foolish," he murmurs, but the playfulness is gone, replaced by a frantic, heavy hunger. He crowds me, his hips grinding forward, letting me feel the hard, unyielding ridge of him beneath the black breeches. "You've been trying for this since the moment you conspired with that...filthy messenger."

His hand shoves upward, rucking my skirts to my waist in a single, rough motion. Cold night air bites my skin, instantly replaced by the searing heat of his palm sliding between my legs.

I gasp, my head falling back against his shoulder. "Vale—"

"Shh..." His teeth graze the sensitive cord of my neck, nipping hard enough to sting, while his thumb finds the slick heat at my center and presses. "Tell me you want me inside you. I shall grant it. A proper bedding."

He kisses me then—a devouring, messy collision that tastes of desperation. He's overwhelming me, drowning me in sensation, using pleasure like a weapon to beat back my request.

And that's how I know.

I know...

I tear my mouth from his, gasping, my hands planting

against his chest. My body is on fire, aching, but my mind is cold and clear as crystal.

"I wish," I pant, shoving him back.

He stumbles a step, his eyes dark and blown with lust, his chest heaving. "Elara..."

"I wish..." To see you? No. He might only give me a glimpse and count it done. "I wish to explore your true form."

ELEVEN

Elara

Vale recoils as if I've slapped him.

He goes utterly still, his chest rising and falling in ragged, uneven breaths. The lust that darkened his features moments ago drains, leaving behind a blank, hollow expression that chills me more than any snarl could.

I expect him to argue. I expect him to laugh it off, or perhaps to vanish into the trees and leave me with my wish ungranted.

But he does neither.

He simply stares at me.

His face begins to shift. Not magically—not yet—but emotionally. A flicker of incredulity gives way to a grim set of his mouth, which then dissolves into something tired. Something ancient. His features seem to ripple in the gloom, unsettled, as if the creature beneath the skin is pacing the cage, unsure whether to rattle the bars or simply sit down.

My mouth pops with sudden dryness as I repeat, "I said I—"

"I heard just fine." He runs a hand through his hair before he lets out a sound that lands somewhere between a scoff and a sigh. "Clearly, I am a fool for you. In a few weeks, you have managed to outmaneuver me more times than the entirety of humanity has in a millennium." He shakes his head, looking down at his boots. "Very well. Let us be done with it. It should be quick."

He steps back.

Then, he steps out.

He moves into the pool of silver moonlight, bony toes barely touching the ground before his entire form distorts. His velvet coat loosens into black linen. Threads unfurl from his sleeves. His shoulders broaden, not with muscle alone but with *presence*, as if the space around him is being forced to make room.

Then the illusion tears.

It stretches upward, growing until alabaster bone and pale-gray skin blot out the stars. Shadows wrap around him, forming a cloak that seems woven from the night itself.

My heart stammers a frantic rhythm against my ribs. His face...

The left side is stark, white bone—an eye socket of

hollow darkness, half a nasal cavity, the jawbone laid bare, a polished curve of ivory ending in teeth, roots visible where gums should be. Behind them, the wet, dark muscle of his tongue moves as he breathes. A thick, ropy tendon, gray and glistening in the moonlight, stretches from the hinge of the bone jaw to the column of his neck, holding the nightmare together with a taut, biological precariousness that makes my stomach turn and my fingers itch to touch.

I squeeze my eyes shut for a heartbeat, forcing air into my lungs. It's just bone. Flesh. Skin. Organs.

It's just a corpse.

When I open my eyes again, the terror has receded, leaving behind a trembling, fragile awe. His jagged skull fuses seamlessly into the pale face of the man on the right, though his eye on that side is a dark pit, half-hidden by a black strand of hair, holding a sort of...sorrow?

"Is this what you wanted? What you wasted your wish on?" His voice is different—a rumble like millstones roughing together that vibrates all the way into my spine. "Are you...satisfied?"

My mouth snaps shut on a gulp.

Satisfied? Not nearly.

I step closer to him, toward a god stripped of all pretense, something ancient laid bare to its mesmerizing truth. Is his pale blue skin cold to the touch? Freezing like the grave?

Death's head turns a fraction, tracking my movement. "You are trembling."

"I am."

But that doesn't keep me from lifting my arm. Slowly. Deliberately.

I reach for where his hand hangs at his side, half-hidden by the night-cloak. It's easily twice the size of my own. Two fingers are long, elegant, sheathed in pale skin. Three are stripped clean, nothing but articulated ivory, bright and polished, clicking softly against one another as he shifts.

A moment of breathless hesitation.

Then I press my fingertips against a transition point—where gray flesh gives way to the stark white bone of his knuckles—expecting the bite of winter, the numbing chill of a tomb.

Instead, a shock of heat burns my skin.

I gasp, snatching my hand back.

As does he, more violently so, jerking the limb away with a hiss that scrapes through the exposed teeth of his skeletal jaw. The movement is so sharp the wind from it buffers my face, and he cradles the touched hand against his chest, the black pits of his eyes locking on me.

"No mortal has ever touched Death like this." His growl trembles like a caving mine deep underground, yet it can't scrape the hint of surprise from his tone. "You asked to see. Now you saw."

"I asked to explore." I take a step back into his space, tilting my head until my neck aches to look up at the nightmare towering over me. "You can't explore a map that's folded shut, now can you?" I lift my hand to his again, ignoring the tremor in my fingers. "Exploring requires touch."

When my thumb finds his warm, bony finger, the heat jolts me again—less startling now, more...fascinating. It's warmth that can't belong to a corpse, warmth that suggests the presence of life rather than absence.

Death shudders.

Probably from how I slide my fingers up, tracing the line where tendon bands into muscle along his arm. Where pale skin clings smooth as parchment stretched over strength, higher into his sleeve, until—

Gods, he's tall.

I strain upward, my boots sinking into the muck as I stretch onto my tiptoes. It's futile, my hand hovering mid-neck on a creature that scrapes the lower branches of the oak.

"Kneel." The word hangs in the cold air, sharp and absolute. "Please..."

Death does nothing. He simply looms, perhaps hoping the logistics of his enormity will force me to abandon this madness. Never...

"You granted me exploration," I remind him, my voice steady despite my own audacity souring my tongue. "So, unless you plan on lifting me up"—I glance meaningfully at the hand that could easily crush my waist—"you need to come down."

A low, grating sound vibrates from his chest. It might be a growl. It might be the clicking of his rib cage shifting beneath the linen.

He holds my gaze for one long, agonizing second. Then, slowly, terrifyingly, the god descends.

It's a collapse of gravity. One massive knee hits the earth with a thud that I feel in the soles of my boots, followed by the other. The ground shakes, dead leaves shuddering around us. His height cuts down, shadows spilling around him like pools of black ink, until his skull levels with mine.

Death's face is inches from mine.

I step between the V of his spread knees, my boot

rustling against his shadowy cloak, a sound that seems deafening in the vacuum of silence. Trembling, I raise my hands.

He flinches as I cup his face, his breath hitching, but he doesn't pull away. My right hand finds the familiar: the high, sharp cheekbone of Vale, the smooth, pale skin that feels fever-hot against my palm. My thumb brushes the corner of his brow.

I search the black hollows of his eyes, the shadows that seem to writhe there. "Can you see me?"

"I see everything," he rumbles, the vibration traveling through his jaw and into my palms. "I see the blood pumping in your veins. I see the fluttering in your throat. I see the bright radiance of your life."

I slide my fingers to the bridge of his nose, over the ridge where the skin tears from the cavity, and onto the polished ivory of his skeletal cheek. Despite the indignity of a mortal petting his exposed structure like a lapdog, he doesn't pull away.

Instead, a long, ragged exhalation leaves his chest as his skull leans into my touch, all but nuzzling against the warmth of my hand with a desperation that makes something inside my chest clench. It's the reaction of a creature that longed for touch for a long, long time. Eons.

The intimacy of it intoxicates me. It floods my veins, dousing the fear until I slide my thumbs inward, tracing the line of his naked gums, my thumb hovering over the exposed roots of his teeth. What would it feel like to kiss Death? To press my mouth to something that is half lips, half bone?

The gravity of that question pulls me deeper into the heavy space between us. My body leans in, abandoning disgust for the dark pull of the unknown. His head tilts, the movement disjointed and eerie, the black pits of his eyes lowering to focus on my mouth. He leans closer, the distance shrinking until his breath ghosts over my lips.

We are so close that I should be choking on the stench of the grave. I brace for it, for the cloying sweetness of rot or the metallic tang of blood, but...there is nothing. Absolutely nothing.

Because he's no corpse.

That realization makes my hands drift from his jaw, sliding down the column of his neck to the heavy, smoke-like darkness resting on his shoulders.

I grip the edge of the shadow-cloak.

He stiffens, his breath hitching audibly in the quiet wood. "Elara..."

"No, I want to see." Slowly, deliberately, I peel the darkness back. "Everything. All of you."

His hand rises, hovering over mine as if to stop me, his skeletal fingers trembling. "There is no beauty to be found, Elara."

"I'll be the judge of that."

The fabric—if it even is fabric—slides away like fog, pooling at his elbows, leaving his torso bare to the moonlight.

I hear my small intake of breath.

Not of horror. Of fascination.

On the right, he's all man—a sculpture of pale, smooth skin and slabs of hard muscle, a pectoral clearly defined, rippling as he shifts in discomfort. But as my eyes travel inward, the illusion dissolves.

The sternum is a borderland.

To the left, the flesh simply...gives up. It sloughs away to reveal the gleaming white arcs of his ribs, an ivory cage entirely exposed to the night air. There's no skin to hide the mechanics of him here, only the raw, biological reality. Gray, fibrous muscles weave between the slats of bone, anchoring the skeleton to the man, pulling taut and quivering with every ragged breath he takes.

"Do you feel this?" I whisper, tracing the jagged landscape of his stomach where smooth skin fights for dominance over exposed sinew.

Death looks down at himself, at the abs on his stomach clenching harder the lower his cloak slips. "Yes..."

The lower I go, the faster he breathes.

My fingers hook into the waist of the shadow cloth, giving a tug until—

Bone clamps around my wrist.

"No," he grinds out, the word fracturing in his throat as he holds me there, suspended inches from...from what?

I look from his desperate, skeletal grip to the fabric straining beneath my trapped hand. Even through the heavy material, I can see the outline. The rigid, unforgiving ridge that betrays him.

"Guess you were right when you said that Death is a man." I don't pull against his hold. Instead, I splay the fingers of my trapped hand, running my nails over the twitching thickness of him. "Can you father a child?"

"I—" His breath hitches, a jagged intake of air that sounds like a sheet ripping as his grip eases on my wrist. "I do not know."

I take the opening. I grip the fabric and shove it down.

Shadows pool at his knees.

Moonlight claims the rest of him.

My breath catches. There's no bone here. No rot. No horror. He's entirely man where it matters, and...proportionate to his height. His cock is massive—thick and heavy, a pale, veined length that strains upward from a nest of dark hair. It pulses as the cold air hits it, twitching, hardening further, yet it is so incredibly heavy that it fails to stand fully upright, resting instead with a thick, bobbing weight against his abdomen.

Death looks at me, his chest heaving. He's rigid under my scrutiny, his body a coiled spring of tension. Black hollows fixate on my face, waiting, watching for the curl of my lip, for the flinch of revulsion.

But the disgust never comes.

"I thought you'd be cold and...decaying." My hand slides easily from the remnants of his grip as I struggle to wrap it around his length. He's hot there. Hotter than the rest of him, pulsing with an impossible living existence. "You're neither."

My fingers curl, straining to encompass his full girth, but my tips don't even meet on the other side. It's an impossible task, trying to hold a god in a mortal hand. So I slide my hand down his length, past the straining root, and lean in closer, cupping the heavy, heat-drenched sack.

Death's head lolls back against his shoulders, a low, guttural groan tearing from his throat. "Enough..."

"Only I get to decide when I'm done exploring."

I fill my palm with him, dense and weighty, testing the heft of him as I gently lift. Death hisses, his skeletal jaw unhinging slightly as his hips buck forward, seeking the friction of my grip. He's starving for this. Just like I thought.

My eyes go to his throat.

Wed him. Bed him. Slit his throat. The words heat my blood, sharper than the strange desire uncurling in my belly.

I tighten my grip, sliding my hand back up the formidable column of him. The motion draws a broken, hissing gasp from his throat, his hips jerking instinctively to meet my palm.

"There was no need to hide this," I murmur, my thumb circling the weeping head before dragging back down the vein-roped shaft. "Could've showed me sooner."

My hand continues its slow, rhythmic work, stroking him from root to tip, and the effect is devastating. Every glide of my palm pulls a ragged, broken sound from the depths of his chest as our faces drift closer once more.

He tries to turn his away, the sharp angle of his jaw tense with desire. "Don't…"

"Why not?" I whisper, drifting closer until the tip of my nose brushes against the cartilage of his.

His groan warms the air between our mouths. "You have to stop."

My lips brush the corner of his human mouth, soft and tentative. He jerks back, a sharp intake of breath, but I follow him. I trace the line of his lower lip until I meet teeth. We hover there, suspended in a terrible, beautiful gravity. He wants this. Gods, he wants this so much that the heat radiating off him feels like a physical weight.

I squeeze him, hard, at the same moment I tilt my head. His resolve shatters. A low, anguished noise tears from his throat, and he surges forward to bridge the gap.

Our mouths connect.

The right side of his mouth acts as Vale would—lips parting, warm and soft. But the left… The left is a threshold of hard, unyielding ivory. My tongue darts out, tasting the stark difference, sweeping against the smoothness of his exposed teeth.

It should horrify me.

Instead, it maddens me.

The contrast of soft flesh and hard bone is tantalizing. I

moan, the sound vibrating against his skull. My strokes slow, growing heavier, dragging the skin of his cock tight until he matches my rhythm with a desperate, bucking grace. I'm lost in it, the scent of carnation, the sensation of bone pressing against my own teeth as I—

Death rips his mouth from mine, heaving. "Enough!"

It isn't just a shout; it's an ancient roar that silences the woods and arrests my heart mid-beat—his clenched teeth, those black pits of his eyes wide with something close to panic.

I could argue that I haven't reached the end of my explorations yet, but what's the point? Looking at the rigid tension in his frame, I'd be arguing with an earthquake. But that only gives me wiggle room, doesn't it?

I slowly withdraw my hand, smoothing my skirts with a composure I don't feel. "Fine," I say, my voice steady despite the rapid hammering of my pulse. "I'll consider myself done exploring, if..."

He exhales, a long, annoyed breath. "If...?"

"If you come to one of the orphanages with me."

His skull tilts, incredulous. "You want to parade Death through a house of children?"

"I wouldn't mind, but I'm sure the carriage would prefer your Vale costume," I say. "Agree, and we're done here."

Death straightens his neck while shadows knit up along those knees still pressed into the ground, the fleshy side of his mouth thinning. "I will accompany you."

Then he rises. It's a sudden, soaring ascent, and yet I see it, the red flutter behind the white of his ribcage. His... heart?

"Wait!" I don't think. Impulse overrides sanity, moving

my arm before my mind can catch up to the horror of what I'm doing. I reach up. No, not up.

Up and into.

My hand passes through the bottom of his ribcage, reaching into the warmth of his chest and straight for an organ that beats wildly against my palm.

Death goes absolutely still, looking down at me with shock-choked eyes. He doesn't breathe, doesn't move. He just watches, paralyzed by the intrusion.

"It's...actually broken," I whisper, my thumb brushing the scarred, uneven surface of the muscle.

"Destroyed," he corrects, his voice a hollow shell of sound. "Hanging on by merely a hair of a thread of my last remaining heartstring. The second, I accidentally tore completely in my rage, while the third pulses in your crown."

I narrow my eyes, squinting in the gloom. "That's not what I'm seeing," I murmur, tracing the distinct artery. "The second string is shredded, alright. But the first one...it seems intact. Strong, even."

Death stares at me, and the black void of his eyes suddenly seems to...deepen? In a blur of motion, he clamps his hand around my wrist and yanks. He pulls my hand out of him, his chest heaving, looking at me with a strange, almost frantic expression that chills me more than any grave ever has.

"Is it... Is it true?" I ask carefully. "Can you really not feel love?"

He swallows. I watch the gray tendon in his throat work, a hard, painful movement. "I feel joy," he says hoarsely. "I feel... some sadness. I feel blinding anger. And... lust." His gaze drops to my mouth, darkening for a brief second. "I cannot feel love."

A profound, aching sadness washes over me, heavier than it should. "What kind of existence is that?" I ask softly. "To live without love?"

Death looks at me for a long moment. Then, his form begins to dissipate. He melts into the night, but the grating rasp of his voice echoes through the clearing one last time.

"A sane one."

CHAPTER
TWELVE

Death

The mirrors in this palace have rarely reflected truth.

They were made for kings who wanted to look powerful instead of guilty, and queens who wanted to look adored instead of doomed. Glass is a willing liar. It will take whatever you offer it and hand it back in a shape you can survive.

Tonight, the mirror in Elara's chamber refuses to cooperate.

The candle flames in this room are stingy, puddled and

dull, thrown from lonesome wicks that my wife forgot to snuff before she fell asleep. The light doesn't flatter me. Never has.

Vale's handsome face is gone, the borrowed perfection mortals have always found so easy to want. A tool. A way to walk among the living without their minds melting at the sight of what I truly am. And yet there's something severely wrong with the reflection before me.

Not in my face.

In. My. Chest.

I lower my gaze and, with a motion that should feel casual but instead feels like a man checking a lethal wound, I slip my fingers under the edge of my ribs and reach into my chest. And there, hanging within the open cage, is my heart.

Scar tissue. Damaged nerves.

It hangs, broken and half-numb, held by a single heartstring that should be barely intact, stretched near snapping in the way a hair does when it's been left under strain too long.

Only it isn't.

The thread is...wrong.

Because the reflection of it looks just right—a fresh, crimson vitality that wraps around a valve that ought to be damaged. It thickens the connection, holding the once near-severed thread together with such strength that the organ barely shifts when I cup it. Worse yet, it gives a heavy, wholesome pulse against my palm.

Once. *Ba-boom.*

Twice. *Ba-boom.*

I freeze, fingers tightening instinctively as if to stop it. It doesn't listen. It beats again, stronger than it has in centuries. How can this be?

I yank my hand out and brace it against the edge of the vanity, cold sweat settling on the little skin my skull possesses. My heart is healing—and with it, the full, agonizing spectrum of the one thing I've avoided since the dawn of my fear.

Love.

The word paralyzes me, skeletal fingers digging into the wood of the vanity frame until it groans under the pressure. How did this happen? When did it start? Weeks ago? Days?

My mind races backward.

Seeking the infection point.

Was it in the grave? In that silent truce when we watched the fog side by side, that rare peacefulness between us so narcotic to my senses, I wanted to soak in it for hours.

Or was it in the tower? When I held her after lust and curiosity were equally sated, and still, I pulled her body deeply into mine. Skin against skin, secretly wishing the sun would stop rising so I wouldn't have to let her go.

Or does this go further back still?

Kael comes to mind. Or rather, the many times his name left Elara's mouth. *Kael is opening up to me. At least he has a heart. He had me on the table by the hearth...* Filthy hands everywhere, ready to melt himself into *my* wife as if—

I stutter out a breath, the mere thought of that boy scratching at my insides like a rusted blade. Disdain for his righteousness, his daring, his constant defiance over the years, I told myself. Now I see the ugliness for what it was.

Blistering, possessive jealousy.

I stare at the red thread in the mirror, the cloak of denial thinning more with each of my heart's throbs. I should have known. The library. The sudden constriction in my chest when I foolishly kissed her. The chapel. The tingle beneath my ribs when I spoke those rotten vows. Those weren't aches of old injury, but symptoms of an emotion long, long forgotten.

I'm falling in love with Elara.

Or perhaps...I already have.

I look at the single healed string, thick and robust, stomach turning more the longer I stare. This intense longing, this terrifying yearning, this ache that feels like my ribs are being pried apart...all from *one* string? One?

Panic, cold and sharp, spikes in my gut. If a single healed thread can reduce a god to a jealous, pining fool, what would happen with two?

I don't want to find out.

Tugging my cloak back to cover my bones, I turn away from the mirror and toward the littered desk. Elara sits there, slumped over scrolls, her head resting on a stack of open books while her brown hair spills over a mouth slightly parted as she breathes.

Her posture is going to punish her in the morning. Stiff neck. Shooting pains. Mortal nonsense that is of no consequence to me.

And yet, I'm already moving.

I slide an arm beneath Elara's knees and another around her back, lifting her carefully so as not to wake her. Any mortal would at Death's touch. My presence alone is something they often sense. Hairs rising on their arms. Sudden chill in the air. Stomach dropping. That instinctual glance back over their shoulder as if they noticed me watching.

But my wife? Oh, she sleeps on.

It annoys me, how safe she feels. As if her life spent digging graves has made her undisturbed by the god who fills them. She exhales softly, curling into me, her hand bunching my cloak in a loose, trusting grip.

My breath catches at the domesticity of it, making room in my chest for the tugging, the twisting, the pinching. My second heartstring, no doubt, frayed ends straining to mend back together in this very moment.

If I were wise, I would drop her.

Instead, I carry her the short distance to the bed like the immortal fool I am for this woman. But when I lay her down on sheets, still warm from the hearth, her arm refuses to lower.

My gaze drops to those little fingers hooked into my cloak, exposing a handful of alabaster ribs. The memory of the woods assaults me, not as a visual, but as blood rushing to my crotch, hot and heady.

I expected her to scream. When I stepped into the moonlight and revealed what most mortals consider grotesque, I braced for the retching, the flinching, the terror.

Ahh...flinch, she did.

But only once before she touched me, little fingers tracing torn skin, gliding along bone, slipping past tendons. She touched me *there*, too, little hand wrapped around my cock, exploring with the same curiosity she used on my ribcage and skull.

No recoil. No disgust.

Only the laboring in her breath. The quickening of her heart. That soft, helpless moan that vibrated past fleshy lips and straight into bone—lust, desire, pleasure braided together in a sound I thought no woman could ever offer Death.

A groan tears from my throat.

That was no scheme. It was real.

Blood surges between my legs again, hardening me with a speed that is concerning. I want her palm on my face, her lips on my teeth, her cunt around my cock, curse and rites be damned.

The need is intense. It floods my veins. And it dizzies my skull with an urge even more damning: to hold her after the way I did in the tower, the way husbands do with their wives.

Eons ago, I witnessed men take their first companions. I observed them sleep with limbs tangled while I rested in the company of shadows. I watched them walk the realm together while I treaded my paths alone...always alone.

I once wanted a companion. I have longed for a wife longer than I have had a name for longing. But that was before...

A shake of my head.

Enough with the lingering.

Having is the first step to losing, so I unhook her fingers, gently lowering her arm to her side. My gaze travels to her crown, gleaming dully on her forehead. My third heart-string pulses within the gold. And within the gold, it must remain.

I step back, allowing the shadows of the corner to swallow the hem of my cloak, putting distance between the sedative warmth of her body and the cold necessity of death.

My hand moves with brutal efficiency. I thrust my fingers into my ribcage, bypassing the frayed edges of the second broken string and diving deeper into the treacherous heat. Where is it? Where—ah...

The traitor.

The mended string.

It feels distinct against my bone-stripped fingertips—

pulsing, thickened with weeks of unnoticed affection, knitting itself together on a foundation of forlorn dreams and domestic nonsense.

I curl my hand, positioning the sharp tip of my fingerbone against the pulsing red of the string. Then I press the point in.

It resists at first, rubbery and slick, before the bone punctures through with a wet *pop*. A soundless roar fractures inside my throat as my knees hit the floorboards, the sickening pain turning my vision blurry. I pant through teeth and tendons, blindly digging the bone hook deeper, dragging it down the length of the string to flay it open.

I tear. I rip. I peel away the healing layers until the red thickness is reduced to a weeping, ragged ruin. Only when the connection is stripped back to a single, trembling fiber do I stop.

I withdraw my hand, clutching the wound wherein the heart stutters, falters, and then resumes a lonely, broken rhythm. The agony is absolute. Excruciating, yes, but still only the faintest twinge compared to grief.

THIRTEEN

Elara

The carriage rattles over the cobblestones, a rhythmic, jarring percussion that makes for a miserable journey to the orphanage. Inside, the cushions are faded but intact, the curtains freshly shaken free of dust, and the lantern hook above my head holds a lamp that lends some warmth to a morning of suffocating gray.

Providing a sense of normalcy, one of the few remaining ministers agreed. A measure to keep the hopeless from piling at the palace gates, a sovereign who goes to an orphanage with a husband at her side. A message to the realm: the new queen is trying to save it, unlike the late king, who refused everything that might save anyone but his own conscience.

I glance behind the white curtain, watching a higher part of Marrowbrae shape from homes with brittle daub and muddy alleys between them. "I think this is the orphanage Kael sent his meals to."

Across from me, Vale sits rigid against the velvet squabs, staring out the window, his jaw locking so tight a muscle feathers beneath the skin of his cheek. "My, my...a man decaying, a meal for the worms long since, and yet my wife still speaks his name with nothing short of reverence."

I frown at him, which somehow brings out how his usually pale complexion seems to have a sickly, grayish cast today. "What's that supposed to mean?"

He doesn't turn. "Presume it makes a husband wonder."

"That's strange, considering that you don't even *want* to be my husband." I scoff, pulling my black shawl tighter around the shoulders of my gray wool dress. "You can feel joy, sadness. Anger, clearly. But I'm curious...what of jealousy?"

"I am Death, Elara." He finally turns his head to look at me. "I covet nothing experienced by mere mortals."

I take him in. The strange tint of his skin, the blueish shadows beneath his eyes, the slight hollowness in their sockets. For a god, he looks pretty mortal today. Fragile, even.

When he shifts his weight under my scrutiny and returns his attention to whatever lies behind the curtain, I only watch him harder. "Are you sulking because of the wish?"

"I am not sulking."

The carriage rocks over a rut, jolting his shoulder against the frame. His hand flies to his chest, fingers splaying against the black wool coat that covers his sternum. For a breath, I catch the faintest hitch in his inhale—like a man pretending he's not hurt.

"Why are you holding yourself like that?"

He doesn't blink. "Like what?"

"Like you've got a thorn stuck in your ribs." A knot forms in my stomach, tightening there. "Is it...is it because I touched your heart? Did I hurt it?"

"You did not...hurt it," he grits out, his voice strained and thin. "The liberty you took that night warrants another spanking to be certain—oh, if only my wife wasn't so fond of them." Vale exhales through his nose, controlled. "I'm simply exhausted. It is the *tediousness* of this travesty."

A sinking sensation caves in my chest. I chose the wrong wish, didn't I? I had wanted to show him my acceptance, to bring us closer. Instead, he feels worlds away.

Abrasive. Cold.

We travel for minutes without a word. The wheels grind over wet stone. The driver clucks and curses the road under his breath. The silence becomes a third passenger, heavy and unpleasant.

Until the carriage lurches, frame groaning under the strain of the sudden wobble. Vale groans, too, his entire body seizing up as his fingers dig into the wool around his chest like a dagger just stabbed into it.

That does it.

"You look like you're about to faint!" A stumbling step brings me to his side, the leather creaking beneath me on the bench when I sit and reach for his chest. "Let me—"

"Don't," he snaps, pressing himself into the corner. "I do not want your care."

"And I don't want to look at your sulky face for the rest of the day," I spit back before I settle my fingers beside his, the tension in the muscle beneath as severe as that of stone. "Just let me touch."

"I don't want your touch, either." His jaw works. His gaze slides away to the curtain and the narrow slit of light, as if he's searching for dignity in fabric.

"*I need your hands on me,*" I mock in a high-pitched voice, words he once spoke in the tower. Then I dig my thumb into his chest, rubbing the muscle, fingers working with practiced efficiency. "What did you do? Did you sleep wrong?" A moment's hesitation. "Do you even sleep?"

He lets out a noise, half groan, half growl, but his hand lowers a fraction, reluctantly conceding space. "Perhaps I would," he grinds out, "if you'd only take a *real* husband, love him, and slit his throat."

"Oh, you're as real as they get." The bite in my tone is easier than admitting the worry nibbling at my ribs. I shouldn't have touched his heart... "Is it your heartstring?" I slide my fingers closer to his sternum, feeling the rigid hardness there, the way his body has been bracing around something he refuses to name. "Here?"

"Yes." The word lands rough, tired. "Mmm..."

Beneath my fingertips, his heartbeat stutters—three uneven knocks, a pause that makes my pulse jump, then a return that's stronger, cleaner, as if whatever was choking the rhythm untangled itself. The tension eases some.

"Better?" I ask quietly.

For a beat, he doesn't answer. He simply sits there, breathing shallowly through his nose, eyes fixed on some point beyond the curtain slit, as if staring hard enough might dissolve the question.

"I..." His throat works, the word caught like a splinter.

He swallows it down, jaw tightening, then forces the answer out in a voice that is quieter than I've ever heard from him. "I fear so."

His hand slides back up to his chest. Not to push me away.

His palm settles over mine just as his head lolls back against the carriage wall. When he turns to look at me, the green of his eyes has gone darker—less moss, more stormwater—caught between relief and something I can't name.

"I shouldn't have reached into your chest that night, hmm?" My admission is a little above a whisper, tasting foreign on my tongue. "I'm...I'm sorry."

He arches a brow. "Pardon me?"

"I won't repeat it," I say, and it's enough to bring a small but sincere smile to his mouth. "If you didn't catch it, all the better."

We stare at each other for a long, stretched moment, the carriage's jostle fading into the background, the road noise turning dull and far away. I can feel his heart beneath my palm—steadier, heavier—can feel the faint tremor in his fingers where they rest over mine, as if he's holding himself in place with that touch.

Then the spell snaps like thread as the carriage slows, the wheels sucking at mud. Vale's hand lifts from mine, his expression shuttering back into something sharp.

He adjusts his coat with brisk efficiency, eyes already turning toward duty, toward distance. "I believe we have arrived," he says, as if the last ten seconds never happened at all.

When the door opens, Vale steps down first, boots landing in the mud with that impossible quiet of his, as if the ground itself makes room. He doesn't look back at me.

He simply straightens, cloak settling, posture snapping into that composed, courtly silhouette he wears so well.

I gather my skirt and shift toward the door, bracing one hand on the frame. I've hauled corpses heavier than my own body without help. I don't need a god's gallantry like—

A hand appears in the doorway.

Vale's.

For a beat, I just stare at it, suspicious of the gesture the way one is suspicious of a wolf going still. Then I take it.

His fingers close around mine—firm, steady, warm enough to jolt me—and he doesn't tug me down so much as anchor me, guiding my weight as the carriage shifts under my feet. When my boot searches for the ground and finds only slick mud, he adjusts without a word, stepping closer, angling my descent so I land where the earth is solid.

"You're playing well at this travesty," I murmur low. "For one startling heartbeat, I thought I had a husband."

His thumb drags once over my knuckle—so small it could be accident, yet it feels deliberate—before he releases my hand. "Start hallucinating virtues in me, and I might be forced to have you committed for hysteria before I demand a divorce from some priest."

Before I manage a rebuke, a woman emerges from a doorway. Busty. Face flushed pink. Apron stained.

"Your Majesty." Her low curtsy almost makes her topple over before her eyes dart to Vale. "And...My Lord."

I look at the orphanage behind her: a low stone building with patched windows and a roof that sags as if it's tired of holding itself up. The courtyard is damp and bare, nothing but trampled dirt and a few crooked benches. A line of small bodies stands inside the door.

"You're the matron?"

"Sister Merin, Your Majesty. That's what they call me. Not a nun, just...someone who stayed. Please..." Her arm opens wide in invitation. "We were not expecting... that is to say, when King Kael—God rest his soul—still visited, he usually sent word weeks in advance so we might...scrub."

"We didn't bring judgment, Sister Merin," I say with a gesture to the driver. "What we did bring is oats. Several sacks of them."

"And how grateful we are. Come." She waves us toward the door where the herd of children scramble. "Sister Margo will have the older boys grab the sacks. Now please...this way."

The air inside is damp and thin, reeking of lye and piss. Straw pallets line the walls, some holding curled children like a question mark. A few older girls stir a pot over a small hearth. They go still when Vale enters, staring at him with an attention that's not quite rational, but not quite wrong, either.

"They're quiet today," Sister Merin says nervously, wringing her hands in her apron. "Usually there's a din— shouting, playing. But with the weather...and your arrival..."

I approach the nearest pallet, the boy in it maybe five. Wet rattles drudge through his lungs at each breath, the straw near his mouth soiled black.

"He took ill only three weeks past. The winter damp gets into their chests. We've given him nettle tea and steam, but..." she trails off, the unspoken 'we have nothing more' hanging in the air. "Death will find mercy on him soon."

Weakness somehow creeps into my legs with such force that I have to lock my knees. For weeks, my sole focus was on Daron. Maybe that's what happens when you spend years with the dead: you go blind to the sorrows of the living. But standing here, smelling the sickness and the stale straw...

My gaze goes to Vale. I don't know, maybe I'm hoping that his eyes lock with mine. Maybe I'll see there's still something left in that chest of his that can come up with enough love, or even just pity, to end this curse.

My eyes find only his profile.

Because he's looking at the boy, the shadows beneath his eyes standing out like bruises. His lips are pressed into a thin, white line, not in cruelty, but in restraint.

Then his eyes lock with mine. For a fraction of a second, the misery in his expression is so profound that it knocks the wind out of me.

Then, he breaks contact.

He tears his gaze away from the pallet and turns on his heel, his black coat swirling around his ankles as he strides behind a few healthier-looking children.

I stare at the empty doorway where he vanished. That was not the reaction of a vengeful god. That was not a monster reveling in his curse, clinging to a grudge for the sake of wounded pride.

Then what was it?

"Your Majesty?" Sister Merin squeaks, jolting me out of my ramblings. "Someone mentioned firewood when they announced your visit."

"Right, um..." Closing my eyes for a second, I call my focus back. "We allocated some for the orphanage to be brought in regular intervals."

"Nobody can afford it anymore with how the woods are starting to rot now," she says. "Once the snow comes, we'll have no choice but to throw the pallets into the fires."

"I know you're doing the most of what you can with the

little you have at your disposal. Trust that you have my support." I gather my skirts, and turn toward the small doorway. "If you'll excuse me."

The hallway beyond is narrow and reeks of damp stone, the commotion of the main hall soon replaced by the faint, muffled sound of voices. What's this?

I round the corner toward another room, which holds only a ragged rug, a few battered stools, and shelves lined with worn blocks. Where did he go? Why did he—

I stop dead in the doorway.

Vale sits there on a low wooden stool that looks ridiculously small beneath him. His long black coat puddles on the floor around his boots.

Standing in front of him is a girl, no older than nine. A mess of curly red hair. Smudges of dirt on her cheek. She holds something up to him, her expression serious.

"It broke."

Vale leans forward, his elbows resting on his knees as he examines the wooden toy. "Everything breaks, little one." His voice is something I've rarely witnessed, soft and gently cadenced, letting a strange warmth rise in my chest. "It's the nature of things."

"Can you fix it?" she asks, undeterred by his philosophy, and lowers a wooden bird into his hand, one of its wings snapped off.

"I don't fix things," Vale murmurs, yet he turns the toy in his long-fingered hand. "I'm usually the one who takes them away when they're broken."

"Oh…" The girl frowns, putting her small, chubby hands on his knees. "So can you fix it?"

"Why would I?" Vale asks, not unkindly, but there's a certain weariness in his tone. "Even if I mend it, little one, the wood is old. It has cracks. One drop, and it's broken forever."

"I know," she says simply. "I still want you to try."

Vale frowns. "If you know it will end in pieces, then why does it matter?"

The girl looks at him, throwing her hands up as if severely offended. "Because I want to play with it some more *now*. Sister Merin always says...she says"—a dramatic punctuation with her little hands—"now is all we're ever given."

Vale stares at her, his lips parting in a silent exhale while mine curls with a smile. He looks nothing like a god in that moment. More like a man humbled by a girl. Or a father schooled by his daughter?

The thought sends an unexpected pang through my chest, a quiet but warm kind of inkling. If there was a time when he longed for a wife, did he ever long for a child? Family? Does Death ever get lonely?

My knee gives a little crack.

The girl's gaze turns to me, her eyes widening until they nearly swallow her face. Her mouth drops open in a perfect little 'O' as she points a grubby finger toward my head.

"You have a real crown!"

Vale stiffens. The muscles in his back seize as he realizes his audience has grown by one. But before he can retreat behind his walls of ice and indifference, I step fully into the room, crouching down until my skirts pool on the dusty floorboards, bringing me eye-level with the two of them.

"It's heavy and scratches terribly," I whisper conspiratorially, offering the girl a smile.

"You're the queen," she breathes, looking as if she might vibrate out of her skin. She looks back at Vale, her earlier demand for a fix forgotten in the face of royalty. "Are you the king?"

Vale scoffs. "God, no."

"Not yet," I correct him. "But I'll crown him my consort soon."

He turns partially toward me, the ghost of that earlier softness still clinging to the corners of his eyes while his mouth twitches a little. "Never."

That lures a soft chuckle from my chest. "Just one more wish away from it."

He looks at me then, his gaze dragging from the toy to my face, catching on the curve of my smile. For a heartbeat, the air holds still. Slowly, helplessly, his lips betray him. They twitch more, then soften, curving upward in a shy, beautiful echo of my own amusement.

His blink fractures the moment.

A strange, twisted expression crosses his face—half resignation, half reverence—as he looks back at the wooden bird.

"You would do better to ask Her Majesty, little one," he says quietly, extending the fractured toy toward me. His fingers brush mine as the wood changes hands, a fleeting, tingling contact. "My wife possesses an exasperating talent for mending things that, by all rights, should remain destroyed."

I take the bird, my chest tightening. I'm not sure what he's talking about, but I'm getting the sense that it's no longer about the toy.

"I'll do my best," I murmur, holding his gaze.

"Clearly," he replies, the words barely audible, before he finally stands to lean his shoulder against the wall.

I turn the bird over in my hands, aligning the jagged edges of the wing with the splintered body. It's a clean break, thankfully. With a bit of pressure and a whispered hope, I wedge the wood back into its groove. It holds—precariously, but it holds.

"There," I whisper, handing it back to the girl. "Fly it gently?"

"I will! Thank you, Your Majesty!" She snatches the bird with a grin that could outshine the sun and darts off toward the hallway, her footsteps thudding away into silence.

Left alone in the quiet, I brush the dust from my palms and straighten. I don't follow her out. Instead, I turn and step closer to the wall where Vale leans, resting my back against the plaster right in front of him.

"I fixed it," I say softly, tilting my head back to meet his gaze.

Vale stares down at me, his expression unreadable, though the tension in his shoulders hasn't returned. "I feared you would."

I take a half-step closer, my skirts brushing the toes of his boots. "You're making it sound like it's a terrible thing."

His gaze drops then. It slides from my eyes down to the bridge of my nose, settling on my mouth. The air between us thickens, growing heavy and charged, like a storm that hasn't quite broken. He doesn't pull away. He doesn't make a sarcastic remark, nor does he say anything hurtful. He just looks at my lips as if they're a question he's afraid to answer.

"It is dangerous," he breathes, his voice dropping to a rough timbre that vibrates in the small space between us. Then, slowly—so slowly it feels like he's fighting his own instinct to flee—he lifts a hand. His long, cool fingers shape to the side of my neck, his thumb resting gently against the line of my jaw. "Terrifying beyond your understanding."

He lowers his head. There's plenty of time for me to pull away, ample time for him to stop, but neither of us moves an inch in retreat. The distance evaporates until there's no air left to breathe, only him.

His lips brush mine. It's not a demanding kiss, nor a hungry one. It's soft, hesitant, and devastatingly gentle. I melt into it, my hands finding purchase on the lapels of his coat, anchoring myself against the sway of the earth beneath my feet.

When he pulls back, he does so with the reluctance of a tide being called back to sea. He doesn't go far—just an inch, maybe two—keeping his forehead rested against mine as our breath mingles in the damp air between us.

He doesn't speak. He just breathes, a shuddering, uneven sound that rattles in his chest. His thumb traces the line of my cheekbone as his eyes open. The look in them is raw, full of a quiet, aching wonder that steals the air from my lungs.

Then, the mask slides back into place—slowly, painfully, as if it hurts him to wear it again.

He drops his hand from my face, though his fingers linger in the air for a heartbeat before falling to his side. "I will wait for you in the carriage."

CHAPTER
FOURTEEN

Elara

Damp earth and leaves scent the air inside the greenhouse, like summer trapped under panes. Above me, the morning sun fractures on the glass, turning into dusty beams that warm my back with such intensity that I almost shiver.

Crk. A dead rose head falls to the pooled skirt of my brown linen dress.

I move to the next stem, the curved pruning knife in my palm glinting where specks of dirt didn't settle yet on the metal. Sometimes, you have to hurt a thing to save it. Cut away the rot and pray the rest remember how to bloom.

Thorns scratch at my wrists in a protest I can respect, so I pause for a second, breathing in the humidity. It's quiet here. Peaceful.

Strange how the silence inside me matches the room. Also the warmth, a languid unfurling in the center of my chest, like a coal less hidden beneath ash.

It's a terrifying, fragile thing. Probably best cut clean off like these dead blooms because...how can I harbor warmth for someone who wronged me so many times? Who lied to me? Who threatened my soul and prowls around my brother's?

And yet...and yet the warmth persists, kindled from how I witnessed a side of Vale he never showed before, capable of warmth, of kindness...perhaps even compassion. Or maybe I just never looked closely before?

Sighing, I prune a stem an inch below where it started to brown, letting the quiet hum around me. No, nipping it in the bud isn't an option. Not if I want to break this curse once and for all, which requires the opposite.

Nurturing it.

That warmth answers the thought like it has a vote in this matter, spreading deeper. *Necessary,* it seems to whisper, curling through my ribs with a stubborn little pulse that feels unearned yet refuses to leave.

I have to love Vale.

I have to love Death.

Something I called impossible, but...now I'm not sure anymore. *"Don't hallucinate virtues in me,"* he warned, but the fact is that he has them. Death might huff a little, but he does honor bargains. More than once, he showed restraint when he could've easily overpowered me. His humor is dry enough to scrape, and it matches mine so well it annoys me. When he isn't busy lying, he's actually honest in a way that hurts. And when he deals hurt? Well, the way he *does* apologize out-skills me by leagues.

I slice through another stem, petals fluttering to the ground as dark red as that heartstring I saw in his chest. Once the curse breaks—once the crown shatters and returns his heartstring—could he love again? Could he kiss me the way he did in the orphanage and feel more than lust? Could he love—

My throat tightens in an unfamiliar way, so I don't let myself finish that question. For now, it's—

"Elara..."

At the sound of Vale's voice, I rise and turn around, a smile pulling at the corners of my mouth unprompted. It dies instantly.

Vale stands beside an iron column, hands clasped behind his back, his body strung so tight the tension radiates across the humid air between us. He shifts his weight from one boot to the other—a restless, jagged movement.

I step toward him, brown linen sticking to my skin as my clasp tightens around the pruning knife. "What's wrong?"

One hand comes forward, clutching his ocean blue vest, fingers digging into the velvet. He doesn't look at me. He looks at the floor. At his boots. At a pebble. Anywhere but my face.

"Another broken toy needs mending?" I ask, forcing a light tone I don't feel, trying to mask the sudden spike of panic in my gut. "Is it your heartstring? Do you—"

"Go to him."

The words land softly, and still my muscles tense. "What?"

Vale's jaw tightens. His hand lifts again to his chest, presses once—hard—then drops as if he's barely steadying himself. "Daron. You must go to him. Now."

A cold pulse travels through my body, starting at my chest and sliding down my spine to my knees, turning my legs into something too loose to trust.

For a moment I can't move.

I can only stare at him.

"Why?" I ask, the word stupid and numb. "He's fine. I saw him earlier. He's doing much better. Has for days now."

Vale doesn't respond.

My fingers clench around the knife until the handle bites into my palm. The sun overhead is suddenly too bright, too hot. Why isn't he saying anything?

"Daron's been doing better," I repeat, louder, as if volume can make it true. "Not cured, I...I know that. But... he's been awake. Talking. Eating a little. Jesting."

"Miss Hampshire cannot find your mother. Your brother is..." He shakes his head. A slow, tortured movement. "He's alone. Elara, he...is waiting."

"I-I don't understand why you're—" The air in the greenhouse thickens, turning me hot, turning me dizzy. "Waiting for what? What is he wait—"

"For me."

The world halts, suspended in a terrible, airless clarity where the only thing that moves is the blood draining from my face.

"No." I shake my head, backing away a step. "No. You're wrong. You're lying. You're a liar!"

"Elara..." Vale steps forward, and the movement is cautious, like he's approaching a wild animal. "Go to Daron. *Now.*" His gaze finally lifts, his red-rimmed eyes finding mine. "I will follow shortly."

"You aren't going anywhere near him!" I shout, the anger flaring hot and bright as I point the knife at him. "Stay away from my brother!"

His face tightens as he grinds out, "I cannot."

"You can! You're Death! You're a god!" My voice is a roar, sending a vibration through my skull that trembles my vision. I march toward him, almost piercing my knuckle with the exposed blade as I shove my fists against his chest. "Do something!"

Vale stumbles back under my shove. "Elara, you have to—"

"Change it!" I shove him again, harder. He hits the potting table, tools rattling. "You told me... In the grave, you told me you can change it! So *change it*. Give him time!"

"I cannot give him more time!" Vale roars, the sound tearing out of his throat, growling with a terrible, immortal power that shakes the glass panes above us. "I already have!"

I freeze, panting, staring at him. "What?"

"When you found me with my hand on his chest, when —" His voice catches, infinite sorrow pooling in his eyes. "When you found me by his bed." He inhales, a shuddering, broken sound. "And then, against my very nature, I did it again a few days ago. Elara, I..." He closes his eyes. When they open again, they're glassed over. "Whatever time I could afford Daron, I wrung out of me under strain. There is no more time left to give."

There is no more...

A ringing fills my ears, high and sharp. The greenhouse blurs. The roses smear into red and black streaks.

He kept him here.

He's taking him now.

Daron is dying. *Now.*

"No. Vale, please…" I beg, pulling at his chest as much as I push and pound, all sense shattering into anxious desperation. "I just need more time! I just need to—" My voice breaks. "I just need to love you! I swear I could!"

The words rip something open in his face, his eyes going vulnerable and defenseless. "Elara," he chokes out. "It's not that simple."

"Yes, it is…" My breath leaves me in a thin, useless pull, the greenhouse seemingly melting and fading away all at once. "Break the curse. Please, Vale, just…just break it."

Vale flinches. "I can't."

"You made it!" A pound at his chest. *Thud.* "You can break it!" Another pound at his chest, so hard it trembles the blade of the knife. *Thud.* "Break the—"

"Stop it. Stop it!" He grips my arms, trying to anchor me as I thrash against him. He shakes me once—sharp, desperate—forcing me to look at him, forcing me to see the terrible finality etched into every line of his face. "Daron will die."

"No! Let go of me!" Panic, red-hot and blinding, explodes in my skull. It overrides thought. It overrides logic. It leaves only the primal, screaming instinct to save my brother. "I said, let…*go!*"

I wrench my arms back with a scream, tearing myself from his grip. My right hand lashes out in a blind arc. The curved blade catches—a split second of resistance, and then a smooth, sickening slide.

A fine, heavy mist sprays warm across my face.

I blink, confused, wiping my cheek.

Why are my fingers so slick? Why are they red?

Vale makes a sound—a wet, choked gulp that bubbles in the silence. His eyes blow wide, shock arresting the sorrow in them. He staggers back a step, one hand flying up to his neck as he looks down at his chest, where bright, impossible crimson floods over his white cravat.

A whimper tears from my throat, high and terrified, piercing the fog of my panic as I stumble toward him. "Oh my god…"

He sways, looking at me with those wide, bewildered eyes.

My hand trembles so violently that I nearly drop the knife. Instead, my arm jerks up again, muscles acting while my mind watches from far, far away. The motion is mechanical, precise, not truly mine—hand lunging, tracing the same terrible arc.

Slash.

The blade bites deeper this time.

More red. More ruin.

"Why won't you just break it?!" My arm pulls back and strikes again. A third cut, tearing through shredded skin, distorting behind my blurred vision. "Break it!"

Vale drops to his knees, hands clutching his throat, only for his fingers to twitch uselessly at his cravat. Red pours down the silk. His breath gurgles wet, ugly, and wrong.

The knife clanks to the ground.

"No…" My legs give out from underneath me. Knees hit stone. "I have to break it."

Vale sways before me, his weight nearly ripping me sideways as he cups my cheek. Warm. Slick. His bloodshot eyes lock onto mine before they flick upward. Above my brow.

The crown…

"We can break it!" I claw at my forehead. Fingers tangle in the cold metal, finding purchase around a point. With every ounce of strength left in my trembling body, I rip the crown free—tearing it away like a scab—and slam it down onto Vale's head. "You and I. Just like you said."

The greenhouse tilts.

And with it, the two of us. Vale collapses sideways to the ground, his palm on my cheek, dragging me with him. We hit the ground with a *thud*, followed by the *clank* of metal on stone as the crown rolls out of my vision.

A wave of dizziness crashes over me. Color diffuses. Light shatters. Everything swims behind my tears, distorting how Vale twitches, thrashes, and gags.

And yet, he reaches for me. The motion disappears behind darkness that pushes in from all directions. But I feel it, the way his wet, slippery palm cups my face, thumb swiping over my cheek before he chokes out, "M'so...ree."

FIFTEEN

Elara

Daron was best with the eyes.

Always had been, his fingers sure, even when the rot chewed away at his nails, working the spoons under with a care that almost resembled love. He was steadier than Mother. Gentler than me.

Still, I try my best when I slide the metal under his pale lids where he rests on a bier, readying him for burial. A quilt lies over his body, thick and plain, hiding the marbling that has crawled farther than I wanted to admit.

We covered him carefully.

We cleaned him as best we could.

Mother's sobs come from my right, raw and uncontrolled, the kind that makes people avert their eyes because there's nothing to do with that kind of grief. "Oh...my son," she keeps wailing, the words breaking apart in her throat. "Oh, saints, my baby."

My fingers shake harder. A violent tremor that starts in my wrists, scraping down along my knuckles before it numbs my fingertips. I quickly break the last handle off.

When his lids sit plump and still, I ruffle his brown curls one last time. His scalp is cold. A cold that returns no warmth, no matter how long you touch it.

Then I look at the two guards and nod.

They move with solemn respect, hands going under the handles, lifting Daron as if he's still fragile, still alive enough to hurt. People watch, gathered in a half-circle once more, a dark mirror of the vigil we held just weeks ago.

Same faces. Same graveyard.

Different agony.

My legs tremble. Not from the cold, but from weakness. A reminder why I decided not to lower him down myself, what with how I can't trust my limbs right now. My conscience wouldn't have any forgiveness left for myself if I dropped him. Not after I collapsed in the greenhouse yesterday, neither Mother nor I making it to his side before Death.

A lump clogs my throat, thinning my breaths. Because of me, he died alone.

As the men position Daron over the open earth, Mother cries even harder. "It is not natural," she wails, rocking back and forth, the green shawl around her shoulders flapping with the motion. "A mother...burying her child. It goes against the earth. It goes against God! My son... Oh, gods, my son!"

The straps hiss as Daron is lowered. The sound is too familiar: rope sliding against wood, friction whispering through the air.

His body descends.

Mother's cry turns into a strangled, animalistic sound, and she lunges forward as if to follow him into the hole. It's Miss Hampshire who catches her by the shoulders, gentle but firm, holding her back from falling into the grave with him.

"He's gone," Miss Hampshire hushes in a low voice, her usual restrained demeanor broken by a single tear that runs down her cheek. "Do not cling. All it does is trap his soul."

That last word lands like a dagger, but it doesn't just pierce. It eviscerates, stabbing into my gut and tearing upward, thinning the air in my lungs until all strength leaches from my body.

"I will take your soul," Vale's voice whispers around me, *"and I will drag it down to the deepest, darkest pit."*

My next inhale struggles past the sensation as I lift my eyes from grave to thicket. Vale stands far from the funeral, at the fringes of the forest near the gnarled roots of a tree. A part of it, yet utterly separate. Uninvited, yet observing from a distance. Present, yet not daring to step closer.

Mist drifts from the shrubs and curls around him, turning his long black coat nearly gray. He stands stiff, unmoving, his gaze set on the grave, blending so perfectly with his dreary surroundings that one blink might make him disappear.

I wait for the anger. I wait for the familiar, purifying inferno of rage to rise and clean everything else out. So I can hate him. So I can loathe him.

Somehow, I can't.

Maybe my chest is too full. Packed tight with desperate grief, suffocating shame, and a guilt so heavy it threatens to crack my ribs. Maybe there's no room left for hate. No energy for loathing.

I just stand there with a resigned calm, a defeated acceptance. The urgency that has driven me for weeks—the goal to save my little brother—has been stripped from my muscles. I am naked in my failure.

How did I ever think I could win against Death? After all this, how could I possibly love him?

Vale lifts his eyes.

They connect with mine across the damp expanse of the graveyard. The distance is significant, dozens of yards of mist and headstones between us, yet I see him with painful clarity. I see the shadows beneath his eyes, the rigid line of his shoulders, lips clenched into a thin, pale line.

Or maybe it's just what I want to see.

Maybe I need to see that this loss has carved a piece out of him, too, just to fan that lonely, tired coal in my chest back into a struggling gleam. The fog seems to indulge me in this foolishness, blurring his edges until he looks less like a god and more like a man standing alone in the cold. Self-exiled.

Why didn't he break the curse?

He said he couldn't. He roared it at me in the greenhouse, his voice cracking with an agony of his own. But how can that be? He created it. And even if he isn't the one who can break it, then why fight my attempts with such determination that it took from me what I held most dear?

The confusion breeds a spark of heat.

Not quite anger.

Defiance.

I lift my chin. It's a sharp, deliberate movement, cutting through the lethargy of my grief. I make certain he sees it. I make certain he feels the weight of my eyes on him, burning through the fog.

I hate you.

He shifts then. His chin sinks toward his chest, almost a gesture of profound submission, and his gaze drops away from mine. He looks down at the grave again. At the first shovel of dirt sprinkling my brother.

Mother's sobs rise into another wave. She cries out, a high, piercing shriek that snaps the tension. Her knees give out completely, and Miss Hampshire stumbles, barely catching her before she hits the mud.

"I failed him," she wails, voice breaking into pieces. "Saints, I failed my boy. I...I arrived too late. I was—I went for a walk. To find herbs. By the time I arrived...my boy was *gone.*"

Miss Hampshire whimpers. "Hush now..."

"No, Mother..." My whole body shakes. Every muscle along my arm quivers as I hook my arm into hers, helping to steady her while all I want to do is collapse into the dirt myself. "It's I who failed him."

We watch the hole disappear, shovel by shovel. With each spray of heavy soil, Mother's wails fracture more, breaking down into small, hiccupped whimpers. Then the hole is gone. A mound of fresh, wet earth rises where my brother used to be.

Dirt finishing what rot started.

Silence reclaims the air, thick and uncomfortable. Ministers. Priests. Maids. One by one, the dark shapes of the mourners detach from the semi-circle, murmuring condolences before turning their backs and drifting away into the gray morning, leaving us alone with the grave.

Eventually, Miss Hampshire releases Mother and turns away with a solemn curtsy. "Your Majesty."

Mother watches her go, then sags against me, her weight settling onto my arm like a heavy, sodden coat. The hysteria has drained out of her, replaced by a hollow exhaustion that leaves her face slacker and paler than I've ever seen it.

She draws a ragged breath, dabbing endlessly at her eyes with a ruined handkerchief. "I should have been there," she whispers, her voice cracked and thin. "A mother should be there."

"As should a sister." I squeeze my eyes shut, the motion hot and stinging against my trapped tears. "Because of me, he died completely alone."

"No, not alone. Just not with family." Her voice is thick with mucus and misery. "Well...presume he's family some-how," she corrects herself. "But it's not the same."

I open my eyes and look at her, blinking through the blur. "What?"

"Your husband."

My throat tightens until I can barely swallow. "What of him?"

"He was sitting there on the bed beside your brother when I came...pale as a sheet, his clothes bloodied. Looked like he'd come from a war, that man." Mother wipes her face with a shaking hand, each of her slow nods making my chest cave more. "He said...he said you fainted and were looked after by Miss Hampshire, so he came in your stead."

My mind flashes to the greenhouse, to the over-whelming chaos of that moment. Everything happened so fast. How I slit his throat, if out of rage or desperation to perform the rite, I can't even say. Probably the latter, given how I slammed the crown on his head.

It hums against my skull once more, my mind going to Vale's bloody, trembling palm. How it cupped my face, thumb swiping a tear from my cheek. *I'm sorry.*

That hidden coal flares up—wild, confusing, against any sensibility—only to be quenched by a wash of cold shock. "What do you mean, he came in my stead?"

"He was holding your brother's hand when I finally got there," Mother continues, her voice soft now, reverent. "Speaking softly to him. Telling him not to be afraid, even though he was already gone. We should...we should have been there, Elara." She nods, a jerky, fractured motion, leaning heavily on me now. "But all that's left now is to find peace in the fact that he wasn't alone."

A violent tremor moves through my body. It starts in my chest and surges out through my ribs, flaring with such intensity that it makes me dizzy. Death can't die, but I know Vale's body can suffer, yet he dragged his freshly bled and newly mended body to Daron? Why would he do such a thing for my brother? Why would he do such a thing... for me?

My eyes snap to the forest.

The space where Vale stood is empty.

I don't know what to do with the chaos of emotions in my core. Gratitude, shame, and sorrow arrive at once, none willing to be put in the ground first. Finally, something quieter settles beneath them all—not peace, but the exhausted stillness of a body that has simply run out of ways to fight itself.

A grave of fierce, painful confusion.

"Your Majesty?"

The voice startles me. I turn, nearly losing my balance on the thin frost underfoot.

The young priest stands there, clutching his white robes

with one hand and a roll of parchment with the other. "Forgive me, Your Majesty. I-I didn't know if I should wait, or," he stammers, his eyes darting between me and the mound of earth. "Your request was urgent. I know this is a mourning time, but..." He extends the scroll, his hand trembling slightly. "I completed the translation only this morn."

The translation. The stanza.

Urgent, I'd called it. Now the urgency has gone quiet inside me, collapsing into a dull, defeated stillness that makes even lifting my hand feel like work.

My fingers reach for the parchment without feeling, dryness rasping against my skin, gripping the scroll like a thing that belongs to someone else. "Thank you."

I give the translation a quick, cursory glance. Ink. Letters. None of them of much use anymore because my baby brother lies six feet under. *Why did you sit with him? Why did you stay with Daron?*

My gaze lifts again. Past the priest. Past the grave. Back to the fog where the oak tree stands stiff and lonely.

But Death is gone.

SIXTEEN

Elara

Death stayed gone for days.

Not in the literal sense, of course. After all, the business of collecting souls is ceaseless. By all accounts of my ministers, my husband has been a diligent god, sweeping through the realm of Issoria with an efficiency that doesn't pause for grief or ceremony.

I spent just as many days out in the biting cold, sitting beside the mound of Daron's grave. For hours, I sat in face-numbing stillness, trying to conjure him just so I could ask why. Why did he wipe my tear with his bloodied hand before he said he was sorry? Why did he stay with Daron? Why is he avoiding me now? Why, why, why for so many things.

But where his wife is concerned, Death remains absent...

A heavy, wet flake sticks to my eyelashes before it melts against the numb skin of my cheek. I don't brush it away. I sit unmoving on the frozen ground, my woolen skirt fanning out like spilled wine across the white blanket that covers the graveyard.

Snow makes the world quiet in a way that isn't peace.

More like the arrest of time, muffling the rot-stink rising from the soil. It softens the sharp edges of broken headstones. It covers the mud where too many feet walked too recently. It hides the fresh dirt, and the brother who lies frozen beneath.

My fingers tremble in my lap, pink-tipped and numb, holding down the priest's new translation, where ink blurs under the moisture of melted snowflakes. I read the words again, their true, unadulterated meaning letting a darkness settle inside me so profound that it feels like I'm trapped at the bottom of a deep, deep well.

To break the crown, love must rise,
Death binding his queen
in lover's guise.
In the bed of the night,
his wife shall yield,
Receiving Death
on the corpse's field.
For the string restores

not by the blade's cruel art,
But snaps only
within his shattered heart.

His shattered heart.

Not *my* heart. *His.*

Kael was mostly right, yet wrong on one part as crucial as it is hopeless. Whatever this warmth is at my core—be it gratitude, growing affection, or even inklings of devastating love—it's useless. It's not my heartache, not my love that the gold wants.

It's *his.*

Death didn't lie when he said he *cannot* break the curse. Trying to draw love from him is about as reasonable an attempt as drawing blood from a stone.

Whatever grudge against Vale or Death sustained me for weeks finally fizzles out, leaving me with nothing but the cold hard truth: I can't blame a stone for not bleeding... and I can't hate a shattered heart for failing to love.

The snow thickens. My red cloak grows heavier. My knuckles go numb. Still, I don't move, watching the sun bedding down on the mountain ridge ahead under the scrutiny of the rising moon.

"Every day, you sit there." Human cadence, not the rumble that shakes bones. Vale. "Aside from getting frostbite that heals within minutes, what are you endlessly doing out in the freezing cold, Elara?"

I close my eyes for a moment, sensing the grief in my chest make room for the tiniest spark, like a match struck on a rib. "Waiting for Death. As always."

Long silence.

"I assumed—" He stops. Clears his throat, a human

sound that seems ill-suited for Vale, and most definitely Death. "I thought you probably didn't want to see me again for a while...if ever."

The vulnerable honesty of his words, the guilt-stricken weight in his tone, touches me deeper than I want to admit. He expected my anger, didn't he? My hate.

So did I.

Perhaps we're both confused.

My neck crackles as I turn my head slowly to where he stands a few paces away, black jacket buttoned high, his curls equally dark against the white backdrop. Snow clings to his shoulders and melts there, dampening wool, his eyes going to Daron's grave before they return to me.

"Death does as Death is." Not even my grief will let me pretend otherwise anymore. "You know full well it was never your nature I held against you." I lift the translation with a shaky hand and reach it back toward him. "And now it seems like I can't even blame you for a curse that simply can't be broken."

Vale steps close enough to take the parchment. He doesn't fully read it. He merely glances at the ink before he returns it to me.

"Was it you who ensured the first translation was wrong?" I take the document back, folding it neatly before it disappears into the pocket inside my cloak. "Make sure generations stay in the dark? Keep Kael stumbling in search of light, hiding that there is none?"

"There was no urging required on my part." He looks down at the grave again, then slowly—almost reluctantly —lowers himself to the snow beside me. "The king who first wore the crown was a cautious, power-hungry... cunning man. It was he who requested the translation be altered, ensuring that any reference to a wife of mine vanished, that any risk of a predecessor breaking the curse was diminished."

"Diminished? It's impossible in its very nature." My throat tightens because, even though I already knew it, hearing it aloud makes it final. "The curse is unbreakable. Because you cannot love. You can never love..."—a gulp—"...me."

My teeth grind together.

I don't know why I said it like that.

The wind picks up, whipping his black curls across his forehead. The skin along his cheekbone pales and thins beneath the rising moon, the illusion of Vale stripping away more with each passing minute. Yet he stays, eyes going to the horizon where low-hanging clouds go from dark purple to night.

I let my gaze settle on the same spot. "If you could undo the curse, would you?"

Vale shifts, angling one leg to brace his boot against the snow. "I cannot undo it."

"I understand that." But for once, I want to understand *him,* too. I pull my knees to my chest, trying to hoard what little warmth I have left. "But would you? Break the crown? Return your heartstring?"

A muscle twitches near his throat. "No."

The answer chills me more than the cold of winter. "Why not?"

Vale's mouth tightens, and for a second, I think he won't respond. Then he gives a small nod—one of those stiff, controlled motions that suggests even he agrees he owes me answers.

"I have walked this earth for a long, long time, Elara," he says softly. "Long enough to witness things that startled even Death. A man, a farmer, who loved his wife with a ferocity that bordered on worship." He pauses for a breath. "Then he found her in bed with his brother."

I glance sideways, watching how his face pales, speckles, a slow revealing of the bone beneath. "What did he do?"

"He strangled him dead." Vale's jaw shifts once, the motion letting flickers of teeth flare beneath those first, untainted rays of the moon. "The guilt drove him mad. I watched him succumb to drink, and then...I watched him beat the very woman he claimed to adore."

I nod solemnly, if only because the story doesn't shock me. I've buried its aftermath—women with bruises blooming like dark flowers beneath cotton.

"Then there was a woman," he continues. "Her husband left her, abandoning her with two newborn babes. She loved him so much, she couldn't breathe without him." His voice fractures, the warmth of Vale's lilt slowly replaced by the hollowing grind of Death. "On a storming spring morning, I watched her cradle them, one in each arm, walking through the rain toward a river churning with snowmelt." Death shakes his head, half of his curls now faded from his skull. "She waded into it, deeper and deeper, crying, wailing for her husband, her love...until the current swept them under and carried their souls straight to me."

The wind howls once more.

A shiver wracks my entire body, trembling straight into the crown that clings to my head. Snow melts through the wool at the motion, sending a damp chill into my skin that makes my teeth chatter. The more I listen, the less his heart reads like a tragic mistake.

It reads like a refusal. Protection.

"When I guided those tiny, pure souls, it occurred to me," Death says quietly, his jacket melting with the darkness as it spreads and folds, "that love only ever brings loss, grief, and madness." He looks down at his hand, fingers brightening to bone. There's no urgency to hide it from me, as if he's too exhausted to fight the truth tonight. "When Eamon died at the king's sword, I merely grasped a glimpse of this agony."

The memory of the ferryman hangs over me like another funeral, quiet at first, then all at once—weight settling into places already torn raw. It isn't my grief, not truly, yet it moves in, anyway, gentling its shoulder beside Daron's like it belongs. And perhaps it does.

"And yet it was enough for me to make certain I would never feel such grief again." Death finally looks at me then, his eyes dark, the whites consumed by the encroaching shadows of his black sockets. "I...I don't want to love, Elara."

Nodding, I glance over at Daron's grave, the sight of the snowy mound making me shiver anew. The grief drives it deeper, a tremble in my bones. Yes, I understand what he means. But given the chance, would I tear that ache of loss out of my chest? If it meant surrendering my love for Daron?

The question summons his voice from the depths of the grave, the echo in my head so clear it almost drowns out the wind. "Daron said that grief is just love hiding in a mourning dress."

He turns toward me, towering but somehow not looming, just a man seated in the snow beside me. And for the first time, I don't experience him as half anything. Just Death, and the familiarity of that settles deep in my marrow, letting my spine curl on a long, shuddering release of tension.

With that release, the last of my strength abandons me.

I simply stop fighting the pull of gravity and sink sideways, collapsing against the warmth of his arm. And still, a violent tremor wracks my frame, shaking me against him, teeth chattering a hollow rhythm as the snow spirals down in thick, blinding sheets.

Death lifts his gaze to the churning sky. With agonizing slowness, he gazes back down at me to the lifting of his arm. The heavy darkness of his cloak unfurls around me, folding over my shoulders to shut out the wind. His arm curls inward, hooking firmly around my waist. Then he pulls.

He inches me off the frozen ground and onto his lap, crushing me flush against the solid heat of his chest, the sound of his long exhale stuttering from his throat. "Better?"

"Yes."

I bury my face in the hollow of his shoulder without thinking, tucking my knees up to make myself small within his tightening grasp. The crushing expanse of grief in my chest begins to displace, pushed aside by a languid warmth. A feeling so terrifyingly close to what I felt once before in the tower...

Somehow, my hand reaches up, fingers hooking into the folds of cloth that pool at his chest, the sense of gravity eerily...comforting. "Did you take his soul to a dark pit?"

Death looks down at me, and a dark, ragged brow knits toward his nasal cavity. "What do you mean?"

"Daron." My brother's name almost drowns under a sob. "Did you take him to a dark pit like you said you'd do with me?"

He lets out a long sigh, his shoulders slumping. "There are no dark pits, Elara. The place where souls go...it has no boundaries, no structures like this world, but..."

A long pause, followed by a twitch in his exposed jawbone. "No mortal word can describe it. It is simply...rest. A return to the all." Teeth grinding, he slowly shakes his head. "I...I don't know why I said that. Anger. Perhaps something else."

I nod, not even bothering to count the many things I said to him out of anger...or something else. "Mother said you were with him. That you told him not to be afraid."

"With or without me, he had no fear." His expression softens into something unreadable. "Because of you."

"Me? Why would—" A sob catches in my throat. "I wasn't ever there."

He tortures the little bit of upper lip he has, bony fingers coming up to comb stiff but gently through my hair. "Daron spoke a lot about you in his final moments," he murmurs. "You always joked with him about death, he said, even when rot climbed his fingers, replacing fear with laughter. And by the time Death came, he embraced me as...his sister's husband. A relative most welcome."

A little cry tears out of my throat, barbed and jagged, ripping through days of numbness. Tears well from my eyes, flooding so hot down my frozen cheeks that each pearl seems to scrape into my skin like a prickling shard. I collapse completely, wailing into his chest, a raw, ugly sound of absolute devastation.

Death stiffens beneath me. Then he shifts with palpable unease, as if the sheer volume of my humanity is something he can't weather.

"I... You should go inside." His hands shift to my waist, firm and resolute, trying to gently pry me from his warmth and inch me back toward the empty snow. "I shall leave."

"No!" My fingers clench a fist around his cloak. I yank hard, fighting the shift of gravity, and drag myself deeper into those arms that somehow feel like the only sanctuary—ever-present and reliable. "Don't go. Don't leave me alone again." I look up at him, his face a blur of smooth skin and bone. "Please stay."

Death hesitates.

His gaze drags over my tear-streaked face, a thousand different emotions he claims not to feel flitting across his features. He looks at the grip I have on his cloak, then back to my eyes. His hand slides from the tangle of my hair to cup my jaw, his thumb brushing away a fresh tear.

He nods. A single, solemn dip of his chin.

A motion that brings our faces so close. Close enough, even the wind slows in the narrow space between us. And in that heavy stillness, something shifts. It's a bright expansion. A warm turn. A visceral intertwining.

I don't know who moves first. Perhaps we both lean, letting the gap vanish. My mouth meets lips and bones in a trembling, desperate urge for contact, a taste of longing and loss, sweet and painful.

For a heartbeat, Death stays there. But then, with agonizing slowness, he pulls back. Not away, just...enough to break the connection, replaced by how his forehead presses against mine once more.

"No," he whispers, his voice thick with a worry that nearly breaks me. "Not when grief is dulling your senses, I understand that much. Best not do something you might regret in the morning."

I nod, the rejection smoothed by the gentle truth, the sincere care of his words. I'm tired, bone-deep. So I simply close my eyes for a moment and rest my cheek back against the hard warmth of his chest. But when my eyes drift open again, the angle is different, revealing something that wasn't there before.

Not like this.

My violent yank on his cloak left it askew, exposing two curved ribs, stark and white. Behind them, his heart beats steadily, a rhythmic drumming that I can feel against my skull. But it isn't the beat that catches my breath.

It's the strings attached to it. The first is as I remember—a single, solid line, unwavering and intact. But the second...

I blink, trying to focus through the lingering tears. Thousands of threads seem to have spun together in a chaotic, shimmering rope of red silk. Only a few loose frays shiver with his lungs where a tear had been.

No...not shiver...

Strain.

They reach against each other, seemingly stretching, trying to mend together. When did this happen? How?

My heart seems to stumble.

What does this mean?

"My wife possesses an exasperating talent for mending things that, by all rights, should remain destroyed." Vale's voice echoes through my head with a strength that seems to vibrate into the crown on my head. *"It is dangerous. Terrifying beyond your understanding."*

I breathe the shivers from my voice before I look up at him again. "Why did you stay with Daron?"

His jaw works for a moment, the shift of bone beneath skin visible in the half-light, as if he's searching for a logic that fits the shape of a feeling he refuses to claim. "I don't know." Finally, he fixes his gaze on the distance again. "It means nothing."

I flatten my palm against his chest, sensing the quickening of his heart. And I'm not sure if he just lied to me again...or if he lied to himself.

SEVENTEEN

Elara

Winter smells different here.

In the gutters of Marrowbrae, snow quickly turned into a gray-brown blanket of slush, bringing out the smell of filth and starvation. But in the white palace courtyard? It smells of pine needles, frozen stone, and a clarity in the air that comes with the chimes of ice expanding somewhere.

I wade through the calf-high drifts, the weight of my heavy green skirts dragging against my shins. It's oddly calming. Grounding in a way that makes me dare to angle my face toward the rare, pale warmth of the sun.

A few yards away, the oddest domesticity I've ever seen plays out on a stone bench. Mother sits there—after I finally forced her out of her mourning bed—her fur-lined cloak pulled tight, deep in conversation with...my husband.

Vale's been strangely present for the last two days, only occasionally vanishing to guide souls to their final resting place. But he always reappears, as if he took my whispered "stay" not as a woman's single plea, but as his wife's eternal wish.

My ears prick each time I make out words between them, but the wind carries them off before I can piece together their conversation. Whatever the subject, it makes Mother's lips wrinkle. Not with a frown, but with a reluctant, fragile smile.

My mouth twitches in response.

Fine. I'll allow it.

I stop in a deep drift near the empty stables and let my leather-gloved hands reach for the white powder out of sheer habit. The brightness at my core intensifies, turning golden, giving a warm, unexpected sheen to my grief.

I dig past the cold crust until my fingers strike something solid. A stone. I pull it up and stare at the gray, round thing. Then I scoop up some of the white powder. Work it around the stone for speed. Pack it for impact. Smooth it round for true aim.

Daron's snowball recipe.

That golden warmth in my chest flares. But it doesn't banish the grief there. It merely changes it into something that still aches, but it's a sweet kind of throb that brings a smile to my lips. Given the chance, would I cut that out of me? Carve the love from my chest? The memories it sustains? The laughs it holds?

Never.

Because love and loss are on the same coin—one side warmth, one side ache—but the value never changes. And to carve out the grief would be to erase the love that made the memory worth living. A thousand times over.

I straighten, turn, and look at Vale.

His heart is healing. It has to be. The tower. The bloody *sorry*. Daron's hand held in his. The grave, and his cloak around me. Each one something Death was never supposed to do. What if Death *can* love me?

My chest warms at that.

What if he already does?

Perhaps not to his full capacity yet, with the third and final string trapped inside my crown, but it might be enough to break this curse...if only it wasn't shackled by his fear. And if I want him to lose that fear? Then I have to show him that grief and love go hand in hand—two parts of a coin that holds the value of life itself.

I look down at the snowball. *Pain is a good thing. Reminds us that we're alive.*

In a sort of excited trance, I wade through the snow, closer toward the bench. I pull my arm back, aiming straight at the buttons of Vale's pretty blue coat—or perhaps that living, beating heart underneath.

Then I throw.

The snowball cuts clean through the air and smacks his shoulder. *Thud.* Snow bursts on the midnight-blue velvet, sending a frantic spray of white across his dazed face.

Mother lets out a startled, joyous bark of laughter. It amplifies the brightness at my core, flooding the courtyard in reflected light from the snow crystals below.

Vale's hand flies to the impact site, his eyes blowing wide, green irises capturing the sunlight as he looks at me in pure shock. "Whatever was that?"

"Revenge for a dozen lies." I reach down and grab a handful of fresh snow, packing it anew, a wicked grin stretching my face. "I'll give you five seconds to up your defense. Five...four..."

Vale glances at the snow on his shoulder. Looks at Mother, who's still chuckling into her cloak. Then, he looks at me.

A muscle feathers in his jaw. The corners of his mouth twitch as if fighting a millennial habit of boredom. Then, a shadow of a smile—dark, dangerous, and brilliantly alive.

"You have a very poor sense of self-preservation, wife." He bends down, his long fingers digging into the drift. "Run."

A spike of energy.

Giggling, I turn, hitching up my skirts and bolting toward the old stables. But not without gathering more snow, twisting around, and letting another snowball fly.

This one misses by a mile. It breaks right beside Mother, making her rise with a laugh before she swats at our nonsense and turns toward the palace to flee our childish game.

"Coward!" I laugh after her.

Vale pushes himself off the bench, sad, malformed snowball in hand. "You'll regret having started this." He stalks through the high snow, much faster than me with his long legs, giving the snowball in his hands a final, menacing squeeze. "Revenge for the dozens of times you wouldn't listen!"

Thwack.

His snowball clips my shoulder, spinning me around.

The cold seep is biting, but the heat in my blood is louder. I'm laughing so hard my ribs ache, a sound that draws shadowed figures to the palace windows.

"Didn't even feel it!"

I dive behind a frost-rimmed barrel, salt-slicked breath hitching in my chest. I don't wait for him to find his next mark. I pop up, a snowy projectile in each hand, and launch them in a frantic arc before I bolt again.

One catches him in the thigh. The other, he bats away with a flick of his wrist. "Your aim is deteriorating, Elara!"

"Don't make me dig for stones!" I yell back, scooping up more ammunition as I scramble toward the perimeter of the courtyard.

Vale halts, tilting his head. "Stones?"

"You wouldn't know what to do with them." I laugh, hurl another snowball, but miss him by an inch. "It's only a thing for *mere mortals.*"

He laughs—a real, booming sound—and shakes his head. "Then you leave me no choice but to escalate."

I turn just in time to see him lunge. He doesn't throw anything this time. Instead, he charges right at me!

I scramble backward, my boots slipping on a patch of ice beneath the powder. I manage to lob one last, desperate ball of slush at his chest, but he ignores it. He takes the hit like it's nothing, his hands reaching out, his eyes flashing with predatory mirth.

He catches me around the waist, his momentum hitting me like an ocean wave. We go down together, a chaotic tangle of green wool and blue velvet. The snow swallows us, a cold, soft explosion that fills my vision with white.

Vale pins me, his weight heavy and solid, his knees bracketing my hips. White powder floats down and catches on his black curls while we just stare at each other. He looks young, happy. And in that moment, maybe he even looks like my husband.

"I don't know what's gotten into you." His voice is a whisper, its undertone braided with concern and awe alike. "Surrender?"

"Never." A smug smile. Then I reach down, grab a fistful of loose, powdery snow, and smash it directly into his face.

Vale recoils, sputtering and wiping his eyes as the white spray coats his nose and cheeks. It's the opening I need, so I shove against his chest, roll out from under him, and scramble to my feet, nearly tripping over my hem.

"Elara!" he bellows, though the word is fractured by how he's spitting snow. "Oh yes, you better run now!"

I sprint for the yawning darkness of large doors, my lungs burning, my heart bouncing. I burst into the shadows of the stable, the air thick with the scent of old hay, dry straw, and the lingering warmth of the horses that went to pasture earlier.

Snow. Snow. Snow.

Where do I get—ah!

From the white sill of an open stable window, I gather two handfuls, my fingers tingling with the cold that seeps through my gloves. I dive behind a stack of grain sacks, pressing my shoulder against the rough burlap, forming the powder into a tight sphere while I wait for the silence to break.

The stable is deathly quiet, save for the sound of my frantic pulse in my ears. *Where is he?*

I peek around the edge of the burlap, my eyes adjusting to the dim, golden light filtering through the rafters. He hasn't followed me through the door, so—

Straw rustles.

Behind me.

I bolt upright, spinning around with a gasp, my arm already cocked back to hurl the ball. Too slow.

A powerful arm hooks around my belly, lashing me back against a chest that feels like an anvil of heat and solid muscle. I let out a sharp cry of surprise as my feet nearly leave the floor, my back pressed flush against the damp blue velvet of Vale's coat.

"Apologize." Vale's voice is a low, vibrating purr against the shell of my ear, sending a different kind of shiver down my spine. His right hand snakes forward, clamping firmly around my wrist and pulling my snowball up until it's hovering inches from my face. "Say sorry, Elara. Say you're an infuriating menace of a wife."

"You cheated!" I struggle in his grip, my heels kicking uselessly against his shins. "You just...appeared behind me with whatever that—"

White, biting cold puffs into my face.

CHAPTER
EIGHTEEN

Elara

The cold is a shock.

I stumble back, coughing snow from my mouth, the freezing crystals melting against the heat of my tongue. And yet giggles bubble out of me, bouncing off the stable's ancient beams.

Vale lets out a soft, huffing laugh. His grip on my waist loosens, but he doesn't pull away. Instead, he turns me toward him, the edge of his heavy velvet sleeve brushing the remaining slush from my cheeks and brow.

I look up at him, the golden light in my chest pulsing in

rhythm with my heart. My laughter fades, tapering off into the heavy breathing between us as his thumb grazes the line of my jaw.

It lingers at the corner of my mouth, pressing just enough to reveal the pink of my inner lip. The playfulness has vanished, replaced by a devastating, raw yearning as he looks down at my mouth. His gaze tracks every shallow, jagged breath I take, before flicking back to meet mine with a desperation that borders on agony.

"Saints, Elara..." He swallows hard, the movement of his throat stark, his restraint a hum in the air like the prickling tension before lightning strikes. "Tell me you truly want this kiss. Say you long for it as much as I do."

Glove pulled from my hand, I glide my fingers up to his jaw until I feel the frantic strike of his pulse against my own, the curse all but forgotten. In its place is an urge as raw as it is old, a longing for the solemn quiet of the grave, the calming fragrance of carnations, the familiar comfort of Death.

"I want to kiss my husband," I whisper, my voice thick with quiet honesty, my gaze dropping to his mouth before rising back to his, steady and unflinching. "And my husband...is Death."

A sound breaks from him, part sob, part growl—a visceral release of an eternity of loneliness.

It vibrates against my lips as they meet his, connecting in a kiss that makes my eyes flutter shut. Within that darkness, I sense the shift. Smooth teeth against my mouth. Skeletal fingers cupping my cheek. Stuttered breaths catching on tendons.

As my palm glides higher, the smoothness of his jaw vanishes, replaced by polished bone that shifts with our kiss. A kiss heavy with the gravity of every soul he ever took, yet focused entirely on the one in his arms.

His skeletal hand slides from my cheek into my hair, cradling my skull with a gentleness that contradicts the desperate sounds tearing from his throat. "Touch me more. Please."

I gaze up at him, at how he stands hunched over to make himself smaller. My fingers slip between his cloak to explore the transition at his sternum—smooth skin yielding to curved ribs—sending a shudder through him so violent that the air trembles around us.

What follows is a slow unraveling of layers. His cloak, black and heavy, falls to the straw. My dress, unlaced with agonizing care by fingers of bone and flesh alike. My shift, dragged down with a patience that makes me ache, the linen catching on my nipples before whispering free.

Each reveal earns a sound from him, low and starving, and each touch of his bony fingertips on my bare skin sends a bolt straight through my center. Warm thumb tracing one breast while ivory fingers cradle its weight. The contrast alone could undo me.

"So beautiful," he whispers, gathering my skirts, stripping the last scrap of cotton from my legs before he lifts me as though I weigh nothing. "So fucking made for me."

My back meets the chilled timber wall. His arms hook beneath my thighs, and my legs wrap around the impossible breadth of him, heels barely catching behind his hips.

I look down between us, and my breath fails. His cock is thick, the grayish-pale skin flush, weeping a glistening thread that stretches between our skin like a filament of light.

"We'll be careful," he rasps, reading every flicker of

concern on my face. His forehead drops to my temple. "Like the first time, in the tower."

"Yes," I all but breathe, reaching down between us to guide his broad crown through my slickness to my entrance. "Slow."

He pushes forward and up, making me clench against the blunt, staggering pressure as my hand flies to his chest. A sharp hiss leaves my teeth. He freezes instantly, every muscle locked, breathing thin and controlled.

"Give me a moment."

He gives me an eternity.

Standing there trembling, barely inside me, his forehead drifting to mine, the restraint is costing him. I feel the violent tremors that run through his thighs. Feel the desperate clench of his jaw, bone grinding on bone.

I exhale. Will myself open. Rock my hips a fraction, and I slip down on him by an inch.

The sound he makes has no name. Broken. Reverent. Older than language.

"Now," I whisper. "Slowly."

He feeds himself into me in careful, devastating increments. A thick inch. A pause to read my breathing. Another inch. Each one stretches me further past what should be possible, the burn blurring the line between pleasure and pain. I bury my little whimpers against his neck, tasting salt on the tendon there.

"Shh," he hushes, nuzzling my temple with what's left of his nose. "Almost."

When his hips finally press flush, seating him so deep, so completely that the fullness pushes the air from my lungs in one shuddering rush, Death goes still.

Utterly, absolutely still.

His forehead drifts against mine again. Bone to skin.

Breath to breath. The frantic beat of his heart reverberates through my entire body, syncing with my own until I can't tell which rhythm belongs to whom.

"Elara," he whispers, and it sounds like the first word spoken after an eternity of silence.

I tighten my arms around his neck, pulling us closer until my breasts meet pectoral and ribs. "I'm here."

He exhales, long and unraveling.

Then, his hips begin to move.

The first thrust is shallow, a careful retreat and return that tests the limits of my body's welcome. Even that small motion drags a moan from somewhere so deep inside me, trapped between warm bliss and chilled timber.

"More," I gasp, digging my heels into the small of his back, finding purchase on the smooth skin there.

He obeys with a groan that grinds through exposed teeth, pulling back further before sliding home in one long, devastating stroke. The fullness hits differently in motion— a deep, rolling pressure that lights every nerve from the inside, making my thighs clench and my spine bow away from the timber.

"Look at me," he commands, his voice wrecked.

I force my eyes open. Those black, bottomless hollows hold me with an attention so absolute, so devastatingly focused, it feels like being seen for the first time by the only eyes that ever mattered. It's terrible and breathtaking, making my walls clench hard around him.

"I can feel you tightening," he rasps against my mouth, his pace growing ragged, less controlled. "I can feel every part of you pulling me deeper."

His rhythm builds like a tide, unhurried but relentless. Each thrust reaches deeper than the last, his massive frame pinning me to the wall while his arms bear every ounce of my weight. The muscles on his human side flex and cord with each roll of his hips, while on his other side, sinew pulls taut between ivory ribs in raw, hypnotic shifts.

I'm trembling, my thighs shaking around him, my hands grappling at the back of his neck. "We have to...have to move..."

He doesn't question it.

Doesn't even break stride.

His arms tighten beneath my thighs, pulling me off the wall and flush against his chest in one fluid motion. I feel every step reverberate through me—each one shifting him inside me, a deep, nudging pressure that makes my breath hitch and my fingers claw at his shoulders.

Three strides. Four. The stable blurs past in streaks of gold and shadow.

He lowers me onto the hayrick with a care that borders on worship, the dry stalks crackling beneath my back as his cock slides free. The sudden emptiness is a shock. A hollow, aching absence that makes me whimper and reach for him.

"Patience," he murmurs, and the grind of that word through bone and throat sends a shiver straight to my core. "For once, I want to take my time."

He sinks to his knees between my sprawled thighs, the knock of bone against stone clicking through the stable. His hands skim up the outside of my legs, bony fingertips dragging lines of fire along my skin before curling beneath my knees and spreading me open.

The cool air hits my slick, swollen heat, and I flinch. Not from cold, but from the first careful contact. Lips on one side, the smooth edge of teeth on the other, pressing a slow, open kiss against my center that makes my hips buck off the hay. His tongue follows—broad, hot, impossibly thorough—dragging a flat stroke from my entrance to the swollen bud at my apex.

I cry out, my hand flying to his skull, fingers digging into whatever black curls I can find there. He groans against me, the vibration buzzing straight into the nerve, and my vision whites at the edges.

He quickly finds his rhythm: a merciless, lapping devotion, his tongue circling and flicking with precision. Every time my thighs tense, every time my breath hitches higher, he adjusts. Slower when I'm close to shattering. Faster when I sag back from the edge.

"Stop teasing," I pant, tugging at his curls, my heels digging into the hard planes of his back. "Please..."

He answers by sealing his mouth over my clit and sucking, hard, while two long fingers—one warm flesh, one smooth bone—slide inside me with a slick, curling thrust. The stretch is nothing compared to what I just took, but the angle, the beckoning press against that devastating spot...

My spine arches clean off the hay as I come undone. The sound that tears from my throat is raw, riding on a peak that goes on and on, each stroke of his fingers extending it by excruciating seconds.

He rises slowly, dragging the back of his hand across his mouth—bone catching on his lower lip—and stares down at me with an expression I've never seen on him.

Not hunger. Not smugness. Something quieter and infinitely more dangerous.

Pride.

"Death *is* a lover," he murmurs, his voice like gravel. "And one not even half bad."

Before I can respond, he's climbing over me, the hay compressing beneath his weight, his massive frame eclipsing the stable rafters until he's all I see. He settles between my trembling thighs with a slick, blunt press at my entrance.

He slides into me easily. One long stroke, my mouth falling open on a soundless cry. He swallows it with a kiss, hunching low to reach me, his spine curving into a great bow that changes the angle of his hips. The thrusts turn shallow this way—short, rocking motions that keep him buried deep while his tongue tangles with mine. I taste myself on him, salt and musk, and the intimacy of it makes something crack open behind my ribs.

He breaks the kiss to breathe, his forehead dropping beside mine, and I feel the nudge of his jaw against my cheek. Then he finds my hand where it grips the hay and lifts it, pressing my palm flat against the exposed ribs on his side.

"Touch me," he says. "Explore your husband."

Not a request. A need.

I trace the ridges of bone, the sinew strung between them. My fingers dip into the gaps, feeling the impossible heat radiating from within his open chest. He shudders above me with a groan that sounds pulled from the earth itself—and with it, two perfectly healed heartstrings that thrum along.

My gaze searches for the blackness of his, my voice thin. "Your heart is healing."

He takes my hand from his ribs, brings it to his mouth, and presses his lips to my knuckles in a loving kiss. "I know."

He turns my palm over and kisses the center of it, tongue darting out to taste the salt there, and something in his black hollow eyes goes so tender I nearly shatter again. Then the tenderness shifts.

He releases my hand, grips the back of my thigh, and

hitches my leg higher against his side. The new angle opens me completely, tilting my hips until the next thrust drives so deep I feel it behind my navel.

"Vale..." I choke out his name—half plea, half prayer—and his restraint finally, mercifully snaps.

He drives into me hard. The hay scatters beneath us with each impact, stalks catching in my hair, on his bones, floating through the dim air like chaff at threshing. The wet slap of skin-on-skin echoes off the beams, punctuated by his low, rhythmic grunts and the keening sounds I can't seem to stop making.

His thrusts grow erratic, each sound he makes more desperate than the last, and I feel the coil inside me winding again, impossibly, already. "Together," I mewl. "With me."

His jaw clenches, bone grinding, as if it takes his entire life force to slow his thrusts as he does. "No. I want you to finish what you started that night."

The world tilts.

His arm bands around my waist. In one fluid motion, he rolls, keeping himself buried so deep the shift wrings a gasp from both of us. My knees find the hay on either side of his hips, and suddenly, I'm astride him, his enormous frame sprawled beneath me, ribs and muscle and bone rising and falling with each ragged breath.

His hands settle on my hips.

A nudge is all it takes, and I roll my hips the way I did that night, grinding my clit against his body. It makes a guttural, shattered sound rattle through every exposed bone. So I do it again. Slower. Finding the angle that drags him against that spot inside me, the one that turns my vision to sparks.

His head tips back into the hay, the column of his throat

bared—half skin, half stripped tendon—and his fingers spasm against my hips. "Keep fucking me like that. Don't stop."

I build my rhythm. Rising until only the thick head of him remains inside me, then sinking down in one deliberate slide that seats him to the hilt. Each descent pulls another groan from him, his stomach muscles clenching into rigid planes.

His jaw falls open, bone unhinging slightly on the bare side, and the moan that escapes is so raw, so helpless, it nearly tips me over the edge right there. "Slow down."

I can't. The coil is winding too tight, my body chasing its own desperate rhythm, each downstroke sending me closer to the edge. His cock twitches inside me, and I feel the telltale throb, the swelling heat that means he's close, too.

"You need to—" His grip tightens on my hips, bone pressing hard into my flesh. Not pushing me down. Pushing me...up? "Stop. Elara—"

But I'm already gone. The coil snaps, an explosion of tingles, and I clench around him so hard my vision dissolves into ringing, shuddering light. The orgasm tears through me in waves, each one gripping him tighter, pulling him deeper, and I feel the exact moment his resolve breaks.

His hands stop lifting.

They slam me down.

He buries himself to the root with a cry that splits the air—half roar, half something frighteningly close to a sob— and I feel him pulse inside me. Hot. Flooding. Each spasm pushing deeper than the last while his hips jerk up off the hay in helpless, stuttering thrusts, his entire body convulsing beneath me like something holy coming apart.

We hang there, trembling, the silence broken only by two desperate creatures remembering how to breathe as I collapse onto his chest.

He shifts beneath me. A small movement, just enough to look down between us. Then he goes rigid.

His breath catches, stops entirely, stillness spreading through him like frost across a window. His hands find my waist, and he lifts me off him with a care that contradicts the sudden, sharp panic radiating from every bone.

Wet warmth spills from me onto his thigh. He catches some in his palm, staring down at the evidence dripping from his bare knuckles.

His bones are trembling.

His whole arm is trembling.

"What's wrong?"

He doesn't answer. His jaw works, and something fractures behind those black, hollow eyes. Something vast and terrified.

His forehead finds mine. Presses, hard, the ridge of his brow digging into my skin while his breath comes in short, shattered bursts. I bring my hands to his face, holding him there, and for a long moment, he lets me.

Then I feel him shake his head. A slow, grinding drag of bone against my skin. Not a refusal of me. Something worse.

"I'm sorry," he whispers.

Shadow curls around him like a closing fist—his cloak materializing from nothing, swallowing the bone and skin and sinew whole.

My hands close on empty air.

CHAPTER
NINETEEN

Elara

I spent the afternoon in a tub of hot water, scrubbing until my skin turned pink and raw. Not to wash him off. To give my hands something to do while my mind tore itself apart.

Now I lie in bed, the sheets cool against my freshly scrubbed skin, staring at the canopy above me without seeing it. The fire in the hearth has burned down to embers, casting the royal chamber in a low, amber glow.

He vanished.

Not retreated. Not walked away. Vanished—mid-breath, mid-apology, his cloak swallowing him whole while my hands still held the shape of his face.

I roll onto my side, pulling the blanket to my chin. The soreness between my thighs is a dull, warm ache that refuses to let me forget a single detail. The weight of him. The sounds he made. The way his hands shook when he looked down and saw.

"There is a...new element, my love. One I would rather avoid, lest we complicate things further. You, Elara, are starting to bleed again."

His words from weeks ago surface like a leaf turning over in a riverbed. With the ghost of his warmth still mapped across my skin and his seed tossed out with my bathwater, the pieces slide together with a click as final as a lock.

He didn't panic because of what we did.

He panicked because of what we might have made. And I think...I think I understand why. It crossed my mind before, after all.

The temperature drops. Not dramatically, just enough to raise the fine hairs along my arms beneath the blanket. A shift in the air, the way a room changes when a door opens somewhere far away, letting in a draft from a place that has no name.

Heel bones click over stone.

Slow. Deliberate.

Fabric thuds heavily to the floor. The blanket shifts. Then, the mattress dips.

Death slides into bed behind me, the length of him pressing against my back—warm skin on one side, smooth bone on the other—and his arm comes around my waist. He pulls me into the curve of his body with a gentleness that makes my throat ache.

His mouth finds my temple. Lingers. "I shouldn't have left," he whispers against my skin, his voice low and rough as unfinished wood.

"No." I keep my eyes closed, my hand settling over his skeletal fingers where they rest against my stomach. "You shouldn't have."

A kiss to the hinge of my jaw. Slow. Apologetic. "I'm sorry."

"I didn't want you to disappear." My voice is smaller than I intend. "I wanted you to stay...like in the tower."

His arm tightens around me. His forehead drops to the curve of my neck, bone pressing cool against my spine, and I feel his breath shudder out of him in one long, unraveling exhale. "I'm here now."

I turn in his arms.

The embers paint him in orange and shadow, catching on the ridges of exposed bone, the curve of his jaw where skin yields to skull. His arm resettles around my waist, and I press my palm flat against his chest—against the open architecture of his ribs, where two strong heartstrings thrum beneath my fingers.

I let my gaze trail their taut lines. "In the forest, when you first showed yourself, one of them was completely severed."

His hand covers mine, pressing it harder against his chest as if he wants me to feel the vibration down to my marrow. "I think...I think they healed because of you."

"How?"

A pause, and then, "You know how."

My heart beats faster, and I look up at him, at those fathomless black hollows that rest on me with undivided attention. "Then let's return the third. Heal your heart."

His jaw tightens. The heartstrings seem to shudder, and

his thumb traces a slow circle against my hip. A touch meant to soothe, though I'm not sure which of us it's meant for.

"You know what the third requires," he says carefully.

"Yes." I keep my voice steady, casual, as though I'm discussing last night's supper and not my own slaughter. "My sacrifice and a resurrection."

He shakes his head. "Elara—"

"You told me yourself that you have the power. That you can bring someone back." I lift my hand from his chest and bring it to his face, my thumb tracing the seam where skin gives way to bone along his cheek. "Just do it. I'm not afraid. And whatever pain there might be...it's brief. I can handle it."

He closes his eyes. Or whatever that slight narrowing of those hollow sockets is, the deepening of that blackness there. His hand comes up to cradle mine against his face, and he turns his mouth into my palm, pressing a kiss there that quivers.

"You make it sound so simple."

"Isn't it?"

"No." The word fractures on its way out. His sockets tighten once more, and the black hollows brighten with something I've never seen in them before—something sparkling, catching the firelight. "No, it is not simple at all."

He's quiet for a long time. His fingers thread through my hair, tucking a strand behind my ear with a tenderness that feels like it's costing him something vital. When he finally speaks, his voice is so low, I have to lean closer to hear it.

"I have longed for you..." he whispers gently, "longer than I had a name for longing. My own wife. My own companion." The words settle between us like stones sinking into still water, letting that gold-tinged warmth in my chest rise. "I have likely loved you longer than I realized."

My forehead shifts against his all on its own, lips straining for teeth and bone. I kiss him, soaking up the connection it holds, how he answers it with no hesitation, no restraint.

"Then let me give you the third string," I whisper against his mouth before I shift my head back. "Let me…"

Something glistens in the hollow of his left eye socket. A single, impossible trail of light, luminous and slow, tracing down the curve of bare bone like liquid starlight. It catches the ember glow and burns gold before disappearing into the shadow beneath his jaw.

"And then what?" His voice cracks like a rock splitting. He takes my wrist and holds my hand against his chest, over the two restored strings. "Say I break the curse. Say I slit your throat and bring you back, and my heart is whole for the first time in a thousand years. Then what, Elara?"

The question hangs between us. I open my mouth, but he presses on, and there's something building in his voice now—something enormous and barely contained, a grief so old it has its own gravity.

"I am eternal. I do not age. I do not end. The stars will burn out, and I will still be here, walking between worlds, guiding souls to what comes after." His grip on my wrist tightens, desperately, as if he fears me slipping away. "But you…"

A knot expands in my throat. "I'm mortal."

"And you will never not be," he grinds out. "Your hourglass has sand in it, Elara. A finite amount. And when the last grain falls—" His voice breaks. Stops. He swallows hard, and I watch the muscles of his throat work on the side that still has them. "There is nothing I can do. No power I possess, no bargain I can strike. No resurrection that will take the age from your body. When your time comes, it comes, and I will be the one to carry you through, and I will not be able to bring you back."

The fire pops in the hearth. A log settles, sending a cascade of sparks up the chimney, and in the shifting light his face is a landscape of devastation.

"You're afraid of losing me," I say softly.

"No. I am *terrified* of losing you." He sits up slightly, propping himself on one elbow so he can look down at me, and the raw, stripped-open expression on his face is almost more than I can bear. "Eamon was with me for two years. Two years, Elara, of quiet companionship, and when he died, the grief—" He presses his fist against his sternum, against the heartstrings. "It nearly undid me. And he was a *friend*. A father, perhaps, in the only way I've ever understood the word."

He lowers himself back down and pulls me closer, his forehead pressing against mine. Bone on skin. Cool on warm.

"But you," he whispers, his breath sawing in uneven waves. "When you die...in twenty years, in thirty, in however many grains of sand remain, I will have three whole heartstrings for the grief to tear apart. For eternity."

The silence that follows is the loudest thing I've ever heard.

I lie there, my forehead pressed to his, and feel the awful, obvious truth of it settle into my bones.

Mortality.

The most mundane thing in the world. I've buried friends. Buried my brother. Carried the grief, yes, the pain...

but never thought of it as anything but a part of life until I drop dead and join them, eventually.

But watching it from where he stands, from the endless, unbroken shore of forever?

"I never thought of it that way," I admit, my voice cracking at the edges. "Dying is so...ordinary to me. Everyone I've ever known has done it or will do it. I never considered what it looks like from the other side. From where you're standing."

I press closer, tucking myself beneath his chin, and his arms fold around me like he's trying to memorize the shape of me through his skin. I feel his lips move against my hair.

"The grief will lessen," he murmurs, as though testing the truth of it. "Perhaps. In a century. In two. But it will never fully disappear. I know this because I still feel the ache of Eamon's absence on boats he'll never ferry." A pause. "And he was not the woman I adore, respect, and love so dearly."

His hand drifts down my side and comes to rest against my belly. The touch is feather-light, barely there, but I feel the weight of what it means like a body straining toward the grave.

"And if I put a child in you today," he says, and his voice is gone, so careful, so brittle, that each word sounds like glass being set down on stone. "If I'm even capable of that. The child..."

"Could be mortal," I finish the thought, old and familiar, yes, but now blooming slow and terrible in my chest.

"And if it is, then it would..." His fingers spread across my stomach, and I feel them tremble. "Would grow. Would gray. Would die. And I would bury my child, Elara, and stand at the grave with a whole heart and feel every fracture of it." His thumb moves in a slow arc across my skin.

"And then their children. And their children's children. Generation after generation, each one carrying some small piece of you in their face, their laugh, and each one dying while I remain."

I close my eyes. The image he's painting is so vast, so mercilessly lonely, that it makes my lungs feel too small for the breath I'm trying to take.

"Eternal grief."

"Eternal grief," he confirms. "Not a single loss to mourn, but an unending succession of them. An infinite lineage of goodbyes." His hand stills on my belly. "That is why I panicked. Not because I regret what we did. Never that. But because the consequences of loving you do not end when you do. They compound. They multiply. They go on and on, and I—"

He stops. His chest shudders against me, those two heartstrings vibrating with a low, resonant hum that I feel in the crown on my head.

"I cannot die," he finishes simply. "And yet, I cannot fathom how I am supposed to survive it."

I pull back just enough to find his mouth in the dark.

The kiss is slow. Not the desperate, consuming thing from the stable, but something quieter. Something that tastes like salt and sorrow and the stubborn, impossible persistence of two people holding on to each other at the edge of an abyss. I cradle his face in both hands, bone and skin alike, and kiss him until his breathing steadies, until the tremor in his chest softens to a low, steady hum.

When I pull away, my lips brush the corner of his mouth as I speak. "It's a shame, really."

"What is?"

"That I'm not the one who has to slit your throat." I trace the line of his jaw with my fingertip, feeling the hinge where bone meets tendon. "We could end this whole curse tonight."

The silence that follows is absolute. The embers tick in the hearth. His heartstrings go still beneath my palm—perfectly, breathlessly still—and then they resume with a strong throb.

His hand finds my cheek. His thumb traces beneath my eye, catching moisture I didn't realize was there. "Could you really?" he asks, and his voice is stripped of everything. No gravel. No command. No ancient authority. Just a raw, naked question from a man who has waited a thousand years to ask it. "Could you really love the one who took your brother from you? Who would one day take your child from its bed?" His thumb stills. "Who will, when the final grain falls, take you?"

I consider the question the way it deserves to be considered. Not with the rushed certainty of passion, but with the slow, deliberate weight of someone who has always felt most at ease between headstones, inside graves, and among death.

"When my sand runs out," I say, holding his gaze in the dark, those fathomless hollows, "and you come for me... I think I'll smile. I think it will feel like coming home." My hand shifts over his heartstrings, feeling their steady pulse. "Like settling into the place where I belonged all along. With Death."

He stutters out a breath. Then he pulls me into him, burying his face in my hair, his arms wrapping around me so completely that I can't tell where his bones end and my flesh begins.

Neither of us says anything more.

I lie there in the dark, his arms around me, and I think about the snowball. The cold crust of it under my fingers.

The stone at its heart. How I packed it tight and hurled it straight at Death, and how he laughed. How the sound had boomed across the courtyard and bounced off the palace walls and filled up all the places grief had hollowed out.

Just for a moment.

Just long enough.

That's the thing about moments. They're only that bright because they go out.

Daron knew.

He must have.

Why else did he laugh the loudest with rot climbing his fingers? Why else did he crack jokes at corpses, and grin at funerals, and hoard every ridiculous, stupid, beautiful second like it was coin? Because he felt the hourglass in his chest. Because he knew the sand was running, and so he spent every grain like it was gold.

Vale's breath is slow against my hair, tingling so nicely at my scalp. He's terrified of the very loss he brings. Of standing at whatever small, unremarkable grave I will get, his whole heart intact, grieving my death for a hundred years, two hundred...an endless compounding of centuries.

I understand that in my marrow now. But outside these walls, children are eating pebbles. Mothers are laying their weighted little bodies to rest.

The rot doesn't pause because Death is afraid. It doesn't hold its breath while we lie here in the dark, warm and whole for one stolen night.

I have to die.

And he will have to let me.

I pull his arm tighter around me. Tuck my chin down. Not tonight. Tonight, I let him have this. Let us both have it, this one ordinary night where we both fall asleep. Together.

TWENTY

Death

The boy is smaller than I remember.

He lies in his cot near the window, tucked beneath a wool blanket that has been patched so many times it likely holds no warmth. His breath comes in shallow, wet intervals, each one thick as tar pooling in my chest.

Heavy. Suffocating.

Still, I sit beside him, waiting on his soul, as if there aren't hundreds of other souls waiting for me. Why?

Throughout my existence, my connections with mortals

have been few. This orphaned boy was never one of them. He's not someone I spoke to. Not someone I watched. He certainly isn't my son.

But he could be. Maybe.

If Death can create life? If Elara falls pregnant with our child? Then I could sit beside my son's bed in a few years, watching him succumb to a curse born of my rage, my pain, my grief.

My heartstrings shiver. Exhaling a breath that does nothing to calm them, I gaze across the dark orphanage. Other children sleep in their cots along the far wall, the drafty room thick with the stench of filth. The matron dozes in a chair by the hearth, chin on her chest, cradling an abandoned infant.

"Now is all we're ever given."

The girl's voice returns to me uninvited. That red-haired, gap-toothed child who had looked up at me with no fear and delivered a philosophy so far beyond this god's grasp. What is *now* but the thinnest sliver of time between what was and what will be? A single speck mid-fall, too brief to hold?

The boy's hand shifts out from under the blanket. The more his small fingers curl loosely around empty air, the more his aura dims—a retreat of life, one sand grain at a time.

Twenty-three.

Twenty-two.

Twenty-one.

"Mama?" The boy's eyelids flutter open, but his gaze slides through me and settles on the window, where frost has etched across the glass.

Fourteen.

Thirteen.

Twelve.

His breathing changes. The intervals stretch, tension leaving his fingers the way the light leaves his body.

Seven.

Six.

Five.

Against the very existence that defines me, I reach out. I push a single finger into his small palm, sensing his hand clench once...then uncurl to the final fall of his rattling chest.

Heaviness settles onto my heartstrings like rust on iron, a dull, spreading corrosion. Over a stranger...

I absorb his soul, the faint, luminous thread that detaches from his body like steam from a cup left out in winter. It curls into me, carries through me, until it expands into the peaceful, vast stillness of all.

A stillness that doesn't match the quiet chiming in my head—the summons of the dead blending into the familiar, colorless hum of obligation. But one note among them is neither quiet nor colorless. Also, not dead.

I follow it, letting shadows extend, stretch, and part.

Then I'm standing in the lower graveyard of the palace. Moonlight lays itself across the headstones in pale, crooked lines. Fresh soil rests on the snow beside a hole in the earth, and inside that hole, waist-deep and gasping, is my wife.

I walk up to the edge, cloak billowing around my flesh-stripped toes. "You're doing a poor job of being a queen."

"It's for one of the guards," she says without turning around. "Took me forever to get through the frost. Everyone else is either sick, exhausted, or too deep in their own grief to lift a shovel. So here I am." She wrenches the blade free and throws the dirt onto the pile, finally glancing up at me from a flushed face. "You look...exhausted. Something happened?"

I open my mouth. Close it.

Elara drives the shovel into the soil and leans on the handle, watching me as if she knows I'm calculating whether to tell her the truth or retreat behind something safer. Something that won't cost me her affection, or the way she slept tangled with my body last night with nothing but truth between us.

I don't want to go back to lies.

"The sick boy from the orphanage." In their heaviness, the words nearly scrape my teeth. "His soul is at rest now."

Elara doesn't move. Doesn't blink.

Yet something shifts behind her eyes. Not surprise—she's buried too many bodies for that—but more subtle, more dangerous. The kind of unresolved quiet that settles between husbands and wives, I've observed more than once, hardening into what will one day become distant silence.

My chest hollows. "Elara, I—"

"I have to finish this." She pulls out the shovel and drives the blade back into the earth with enough force to split the stones beneath. The crack echoes across the graveyard.

I watch her work for a moment. The vicious rhythm of it. The way each *hrrk* seems to lift out a grave for our marriage, sending a clawed scrape down my spine.

I jump into the grave with her. The space is cramped, the shovel small. My looming height forces me to hunch, my bones clicking as I wrap my knuckles around the handle.

I shake my head. "You don't understand."

Elara steps back against the earthen wall, arms folding

across her chest, and watches me with an expression I cannot read. "I do understand."

"No." I drive the shovel down harder than necessary. The blade clangs against rock, and the impact jolts up through my wrists. "You have—what, sixty years? Seventy? A blink in the span of my existence. What would someone so temporary understand of eternity?"

The words land badly, I know it the moment they leave my mouth. Know it by the way her chin lifts, by the way her arms tighten across her chest, by the barely perceptible anger she tries to bury beneath the dirt on her face.

"But I know what *this* feels like." The words snap out of her, hand gesturing between the narrow grave, the frozen dirt, the impossible distance between us contained in three feet of space. "And I do understand. Just because—" She clenches her eyes shut. Presses her fingers against her temples. When she speaks again, the edge is gone, replaced by something more ragged. "I'm sorry. I shouldn't have... I'm exhausted. I've been digging this grave for three hours in frozen soil, and I just—"

She stops. Breathes. Opens her eyes and looks at me, and beneath the frustration and the dirt and the dark circles carved under her eyes, there is something tender and fraying.

"You're exhausted, too," she says softly. "I can see it."

I scoff. I'm not sure if exhaustion is the right word for the particular weariness of an immortal arguing with his mortal wife about whether love is worth the pain it guarantees.

I lean on the shovel. Say nothing.

Elara is quiet for a long moment. When she speaks again, her voice is shifted—no longer sharp, no longer snapping, but careful. Deliberate. The voice of a woman choosing her words the way she chooses where to place a headstone: with precision, because once it's set, it doesn't move.

"What did you think was going to happen?" she asks. "After last night. After everything we said to each other." She searches my face. "Did you think I would just...accept this? Wake up beside you and agree to watch the rot spread and the realm die?"

My jawbone gives a tight, weary pop. "I...did not think that far in the moment."

"Neither of us did." She leans back against the grave wall again, tilting her head to look up at the stars above us. "But the moment is over, and the rot is still here, and people are still dying, and I'm standing in a grave I dug alone because there's no one left who is well enough to help me."

She looks back at me.

"I understand, Vale." Her voice cracks on my name. The name I bestowed upon myself, but the way she says it...as though it has become something more personal than any name she's ever spoken. "I have compassion for your fear. I understand the weight of grief. But understanding why you refuse doesn't mean I support it. Not when the cost is..." She gestures above us, at the graveyard, at the palace beyond, at all of it. "This. All of this."

Something behind my ribs lurches—a visceral, ugly thing, like a hand closing around my heartstrings and *twisting*. "What are you saying?"

Her arms squeeze across her chest, a silent conflict playing out across her face. How she drops her gaze to the dirt between us, then lifts to a headstone nearby, then finally, reluctantly, settles on me.

"Maybe you were right," she whispers. "Maybe we should divorce."

Another twist, stopping the blood in my heart until it cools into the familiar numbness of years passed. "I beg your pardon."

"If I can't break the curse," she continues, each word sounding like it's being pulled from her by force, "then I have to feed it. And to feed it, I need a husband." She swallows. "A real one. Like you said."

Like I said...

The memory surfaces with sickening clarity: me telling her to find a husband she could love. A mortal man. Someone with a lifespan and the biological capacity to die with her. It had been *my* suggestion. My strategic, reasonable, perfectly logical suggestion, delivered with the cold efficiency of a god who'd not yet remembered how to long.

I remember now. Painfully.

Jealousy hits with a blinding flare behind my sternum, followed by rage at the faceless man who would dare to hold her in my stead. "I refuse."

Elara scoffs. A short, sharp breath through her nose that clouds white in the frozen air. "Do you love me yet?"

I only stare at her, the words awfully familiar, yet making no sense. "What?"

"You refuse to let me go." She steps forward, and the grave narrows to nothing between us. "Trapping me in a marriage that forces me to watch the world die. How is that love?"

The pressure builds behind my sternum like a clenching fist, wrenching a shout from my chest. "You are trying to force my hand!"

"I'm not forcing you to do anything!" Her voice rises to match mine, then catches, trembles, steadies. "But neither will I force myself to indulge in a love—however real, however *wanted*—when it's costing me my conscience."

"And what will it cost *me*?" The word tears out of me raw and ragged, ricocheting off the earthen walls, startling a crow from a nearby tree. "I would die for you!" The words come out low and wrecked and shaking. "If I could, I would die for you."

The silence stretches between us like the night itself holds its breath.

Then Elara exhales. Slow. Measured. "Dying for someone is easy."

The words are quiet, almost gentle. Which makes them worse.

"You know that better than anyone." She gestures at me, all of me, every tendon and bone. "You've gathered their souls. The mothers who threw themselves over cradles. The soldiers who stepped in front of swords. The old men who gave their last scrap of bread and called it enough." She pauses. "And I know it, too, because I'm the one who buried what you left behind."

Her eyes hold mine, steady and unblinking.

"We both know dying is easy. It's a single moment. One decision, and then...it's done. And you never have to feel the weight of what comes after." She tilts her head. "But *living* for someone? Waking up every morning, even when it hurts, even when you can't fathom to keep going?" The corner of her mouth twitches. "Try that. If you want to impress me."

Something cracks in my chest. Not the heartstrings. Something deeper. Something...structural.

"And if there's a child." My voice comes out hoarse. "*Our* child. I will love it. I will hold it. I will watch it grow and stumble and become something extraordinary, and then one day—one day, Elara—I will watch it die. And then their children. And—"

"Stop."

The word is firm but not cruel. Elara reaches up and presses her dirt-caked hand against my chest, directly over the place where the heartstrings ache.

"Every headstone marks someone who would cherish what you're afraid of." Her fingers curl into the fabric of my cloak. "Somewhere in a graveyard, there's a woman who never met her grandson. A father who died the winter before his daughter's wedding."

A tremor runs through my sternum, sharp enough to make me wince. "Elara..."

"They would give everything just to see one wobbly first step. One wiggly milk tooth pressed into their palm. To watch their child fall madly, stupidly in love." Rough and calloused, her palm strokes up along the tendon on my neck, only to cup my jawbone. "You looked so happy yesterday during the snowball fight. Were you? Happy?"

My jaw works. I don't even recall when I was last this happy, if ever. "Yes."

"None of it would've happened had you turned down the joy over the sadness that the snow will melt, eventually." Tears streak through the dirt on her cheeks, but her voice holds. "You can't have love without embracing grief. Pain is the price we pay for participating in life. And if you're not willing to pay that, then maybe..." Her other hand finds the exposed curve of my sternum, fingers slipping around the bone to rest against the heat. "Then maybe you're a corpse after all. Existing somehow, yes. But not living."

The words don't just land. They excavate. They dig past

tendons and sinew, past ancient bone and godly power, and find the soft, trembling heart that falters in my chest.

Shovel pulled from the ground, she turns her back on me and drives the iron into the dirt. "I have to finish this."

I stand there, as unmoving as the dead, the shovel biting into the earth with a *hrrk* that reverberates through the soles of my feet, up through my anklebones, my shins, settling into the marrow like a burial hymn.

I'm standing in my own grave.

TWENTY-ONE

Elara

Something tickles my hair. A faint, rhythmic stroke. Featherlight. Barely there.

It pulls me from sleep the way dawn pulls mist from a lake. Slow. Gradual. One sense at a time. First touch. Then the quiet exhale of a breath that isn't mine. The scent of carnations follows, drifting into my nose with hints of soil and snow.

I open my eyes.

Vale sits on the floor beside my bed, his back against the frame, his long legs folded at impractical angles. One hand rests on his knee, while the other gently combs through the loose strands of my hair splayed across the pillow.

I clear the roughness of sleep from my voice. "How long have you been here?"

He continues the slow, absent drag through tangles, watching me with those green eyes that hold too much for one morning. "A while."

I search his face. Pale. Shadows pooled beneath his lashes. The stubborn set of his jaw softer than usual, as though the night chewed on him and spat out what was left.

"I want it noted," he says, his voice low, the gravel of it catching on something fragile, "that I am not fully convinced."

"Convinced of what?"

He shifts, rising to his knees beside the bed. His hand leaves my hair and finds my cheek instead, cradling it with a careful, trembling pressure that turns my face toward his until the green of his eyes is all I see.

"You were right. In the grave. About all of it." His jaw works, a muscle feathering beneath the skin. "I have to choose before life chooses for me. And there are only two paths."

He's quiet for a long moment. When he speaks again, his voice is lower. Rougher. "I break the curse. Mend the third string. Feel everything—every death, every loss, the full, annihilating weight of your eventual absence—with a whole and unprotected heart." A pause, heavy as wet soil. "Or I refuse. Watch resentment curdle between us. Watch you walk away. Watch another man gain your heart. Lose you not to mortality..." His throat works once, hard. "But to a life I was too afraid to choose."

The air leaves my lungs in a rush that has no part in

breathing. I stare at him, my pulse suddenly loud enough to hear in my skull, my fingers twisting the edge of the blanket into a knot. "You mean...?"

His forehead drops against mine. "Both paths end in pain; I understand that now." Something shifts in those green eyes. A deepening, as if the man himself is looking at me harder. "Between the two, I choose the one that allows me to do life with you until then."

The words land in the center of my chest. There they cave, joy splitting through me first. Hot. Golden. Blinding. Fear follows, a terror so sharp it makes my throat lock up because...he agreed to kill me.

I don't speak. I can't. Instead, I reach for him, hands finding his jaw, pulling his mouth down to mine.

The kiss is slow at first. Trembling. Tasting of salt and the sleepless hours behind his eyes. His hand slides from my cheek into my hair, cradling my skull, and the low, broken sound he makes against my lips undoes something in my chest.

I pull him closer. He resists for half a heartbeat, then gives, his weight sinking onto the edge of the bed, one knee pressing into the mattress beside my hip. The blanket is still tangled around my legs, and I kick at it blindly, needing the barrier gone, needing less between us.

His mouth finds the hollow of my throat, where he whispers, "I love you."

My head falls back against the pillow, fingers raking through those black curls, and the sound I make is neither brave nor queenly. It's the sound of a woman who almost lost this. A woman who is still terrified of what comes next but refuses to waste the now on fear.

"Elara..." He breathes my name into my collarbone, his lips dragging a slow, devastating line toward my shoulder.

His hand finds my hip through the thin shift, gripping hard, pulling me flush against him.

Heat builds between us with a speed that's almost violent. Weeks of grief and argument and longing compressed into the urgent crush of his mouth, the slide of his palm up my thigh, the way my back arches off the bed to chase the friction. I hook my leg around his hip and feel him—hard, straining, his breath hitching into something ragged against my skin.

My fingers fumble with the buttons of his coat. One. Two. My hand slips beneath, finding the warm, solid expanse of his chest, and his entire body shudders.

"I want you," I whisper against his mouth. "Before we do this. I need—"

"No." He pulls back.

Not far. Just enough to look at me, his chest heaving, his pupils blown so wide the green is barely a ring. His hand is still on my thigh, trembling with the effort of stopping.

"If I have you now," he says, his voice wrecked, "there's no force in this realm or any other that will make me slit your throat after."

The honesty of it lands like a fist. Not cruelty. Not denial. Just the raw, terrified truth of a man who knows the gore of what will come next.

I close my eyes. Breathe. Let the heat settle into something I can carry rather than something that consumes.

"Then we should go," I whisper. "Before we both change our minds."

He exhales a long, unraveling breath and presses his lips to my forehead. They linger there. One second. Three. Five. As though he's memorizing the feel of my skin.

"I already told Miss Hampshire to ready the blade."

"Oh…" My stomach drops. "You thought this through, huh?"

"Would you like to eat first?" He studies me, head tilted, as though genuinely considering the logistics of a pre-sacrifice breakfast. "Find an appropriate dress?"

I sit up, the shift falling off one shoulder where his mouth had pushed it. "Who eats breakfast before their slaughter?" I shove the blanket off my legs. "And no dress is appropriate if it'll get bloodied, anyway."

That softening in his jaw again. That almost-smile that's become my favorite thing on his borrowed, stupidly handsome face. "Indeed."

Before my feet find the cold floor, his arms are under me. One beneath my knees, the other cradling my back, lifting me from the bed with ease. I loop mine around his neck, pressing my cheek to his shoulder, and I can feel the faint vibration of his heartstrings humming against me.

Two strings. Soon to be three.

"I just want to hold you for a while," Vale says, carrying me through the doorway, the hallway beyond pale and still.

A maid rounds the corner, sees the king carrying his queen, who is wearing only a nightgown, and flattens herself against the wall with a clumsy curtsy. Vale nods at her as though it's perfectly ordinary.

I press closer to him. "I'm scared."

His lips find my temple. "Whatever happened to 'Dying is easy,' my love?"

A startled laugh escapes me, bright and too loud, echoing off the stone and coming back sounding almost like courage. "Shut up."

It starts in my hands, that tremble when the double doors of the throne room loom ahead. Travels inward. Coils behind my sternum until breathing becomes impossible.

Dizziness fogs my mind, whirling up those first roots of panic.

I dig my fingers into his coat. "Put me down."

He stops and looks at me. No hurt. No offense. Just patience.

"I just..." A shallow, almost hiccupped breath. "I have to walk."

He sets me down, my bare soles meeting the shock of cold stone, and extends his hand. I take it. He laces his fingers through mine, and we walk the final stretch together. Not leading. Not following. Side by side.

The doors groan open.

The throne room is empty. Just the long stretch of marble, the vaulted ceiling, the colored light from the high windows falling across the floor in pale, fractured shapes.

And Miss Hampshire, beside the throne, the cloth-wrapped blade cradled in her arms. "Your Majesty."

The cloth falls away. Steel catches the morning light and throws a sliver of pink across the floor. My throat narrows, eyes going to the spot where Kael's blood pooled not so long ago. Scrubbed. Sanded. Oiled.

But my feet know where it was.

Where mine will be.

"Should I fetch your mother?" Miss Hampshire asks.

"No." Too fast. I soften it. "If this works, then there's nothing to explain. And if it doesn't..." I glance at Vale. "No need to frighten her with something she'll never have to grieve."

Miss Hampshire sets the blade on the arm of the throne.

I turn to Vale. "You can bring me back."

"Yes." His thumb traces a circle against my knuckle. "I've done it once. A woman startled at the sight of me, slipped, hit her head. Died hours later. Years too soon." A muscle shifts in his jaw. "I set it right. As I will set this right."

Miss Hampshire rests her hand on my shoulder. "Breathe, child."

"Right..." I look at the blade. "Let's do it."

Vale lifts the steel from the velvet and turns to me. "Take off your crown. You must place it on my head." His eyes hold mine, green and steady and full of something too tender for this room. "Crown me yours, Elara. Because I am, and I will never again not be."

My fingers rise to the circlet. The metal hums as I lift it free, almost as if it knows. It leaves a phantom weight behind, a ghost of pressure, as I step forward, rise onto my toes, and settle the crown onto his dark curls.

"Nobody is here but us," I whisper. "I need to see your heart when we do this. Please."

Vale places a whisper-soft kiss to my temple. "You will have me in whichever form you request."

The shift moves through him like a shudder. Vale falls away; Death rises through. Miss Hampshire inhales sharply behind me—a single step backward, shoe scraping stone.

"I could have done without ever having to see this again," she mutters.

Death parts his cloak. Ribs. Sinew. And there...his heart, two strings pulsing, a ragged absence where the third should be. "Are you ready?"

My eyes burn. I nod.

He raises the blade to my throat. Then stops.

His hand trembles. Not a faint tremor, but a shudder that moves through his entire arm, rattling bone against tendon, making the steel quiver so violently the light dances off it like something panicked.

He pulls the blade back. Stares at it. Then brushes his

cloak up and draws the edge across his forearm. A thin dark line opens, weeping something too thick and too slow to be blood. He watches it bead, testing sharpness, learning depth.

"It's sharp," I say. "Whatever pain there is, I can handle—"

"Don't." The word is ragged. "Talk of pain, and I will stop. And I cannot stop."

I close my mouth.

He returns the blade to my throat. Steel kisses skin, cold enough to make every nerve skitter awake. His other hand cradles the back of my head, bony fingertips threading into my hair, drawing me forward until his forehead presses against mine.

Bone to skin. Endless to mortal.

The blade ceases to exist. There's only this: his breath on my lips, the pulse of his heart, the two remaining strings visibly shivering.

"Elara." My name has never sounded like that before. Like a prayer from someone who has never prayed. "Say it. Say you love me."

"I love you." The words come as easily as breathing. "I'm yours. I was probably born yours."

"And I love you." Gold softens against the ridges of his skull, beading into slow, molten pearls that trace the hollows of bone the way tears trace a cheek. One trails down his temple, pools in the socket of his eye, slides along the edge of his jaw, and hangs there. Trembling. Refusing to fall. "Will love you until the day I die."

His lips press against mine. Dry. Trembling. Tasting of frost and carnations and ancient, aching loneliness.

The kiss deepens. Just enough.

Then the blade bites.

Heat slams into my throat, a deep burn that wraps around something thick, something choking. Copper floods my mouth, sweet and warm, bubbling onto the back of my tongue. My hands fly to the slick heat on my neck. The world tilts. My legs dissolve, and I can't breathe.

I can't—

Oh my god, I can't breathe!

Death rips his mouth from mine on a sound that isn't a scream. It's worse. Lower. The kind of noise that comes from a chest being split open from the inside. His knees hit the ground, his arms ripping me down with him.

And yet he cradles me against him as he takes the fall, absorbing the impact the way the earth absorbs a body.

My cheek hits his chest. Through the blur, through the dark pressing in from every edge, I see it.

Gold slides between the open slats of his ribs. Molten. Slow. It drips onto his heart and stretches, pulling long and thin and taut, spinning itself into a thread that pulses once, twice...then holds. Three strings. The third brighter than the others, burning with a newness that hurts to look at.

His trembling palm finds my cheek, smearing thick dampness across it as his mouth moves. I can't hear him.

The throne room dims. The vaulted ceiling folds inward. Miss Hampshire's silhouette shrinks to a pinprick before it vanishes, and everything collapses into a tunnel that narrows around the only thing still shining.

His heart. Pulsing like a lantern held up in a storm.

I follow it. Not because I choose to. It's the only direction left. It pulls me gently, warmly, the way a current pulls a leaf, and the farther I drift, the quieter everything becomes. No pain. No copper. No choking. Just a vast, humming stillness that settles into me the way soil folds over a grave.

It feels like the space between headstones on a summer evening. Like the quiet after a burial, when even the wind holds its tongue. It feels like the place I've always belonged, among the silent, the still.

Among death.

Then...a sound.

Distant. Wrecked. A voice dragged across gravel and broken glass, shaping itself around three familiar syllables. "Elara..."

It isn't a summons. It's a sob. The kind of sound I've heard a thousand times at gravesides, the grief of someone who isn't ready to let go.

"Come back to me."

The light holds. Warm. Perfect. Infinite.

But that sob...

It hooks into something I no longer have, somewhere below the light, below the peace. It pulls. Neither hard nor violent. Just a steady, aching tug, like a hand reaching into deep water and closing around my wrist with the grip of a man who refuses to let go.

"I will not allow you through." The light shudders. "You asked me to live. Now come back and live with me."

Another sob.

I turn toward it. Toward the endless, terrifying vastness of black unknowing. As unpredictable as life itself, and yet I take a blind step toward it. Cold rushes in from below, biting and rough. It yanks me down, making me plummet back into weight, into breath...

...into the raw uncertainty of life.

CHAPTER
TWENTY-TWO

Elara

Warmth.

Not the sharp, immediate warmth of a hearth or a hot bath, but something deeper. Slower. The kind that seeps into your bones from a body pressed against yours, steady and unhurried, as if it's been there for a long time and has no plans to leave.

My cheek rests on something solid. Rising. Falling. Rising again. A rhythm so slow and heavy it barely qualifies as breathing, each exhale a low, rumbling vibration that hums through my skull like a lullaby.

I know this chest.

My fingers twitch against soft velvet, and beneath it, the unmistakable beat of a heart. Rhythmic. Strong. Whole.

My eyes flutter open, awareness settling on the lightness of my head. The crown is gone. My scalp bare. Naked. No hum, no bite, no cold metallic gnaw. Just skin and hair and the faint ghost of something that left not long ago.

I turn my head.

Vale's eyes are firmly closed. He's asleep. Truly, deeply asleep, his lips slightly parted, his lashes dark crescents against skin that looks less pale than usual. Less drawn. The shadows beneath his eyes have not vanished exactly, but thinned.

I've never seen him like this.

Still, yes. He can be still as a headstone when he wants. But this is different. This isn't the coiled, watchful stillness of a predator deciding whether to strike. This is surrender. The deep, boneless collapse of a body that hasn't properly rested in longer than I can fathom, finally given permission to rest.

A soft, rhythmic clicking draws my ear sideways.

Mother sits in a chair beside the bed, a ball of gray wool in her lap and two wooden needles working a steady, unhurried rhythm. *Click-click. Click-click.* The sound is so domestic, so absurdly normal that, for a disorienting moment, I think I'm back in our old house, small and feverish, waking from some childhood illness to find her keeping watch.

"There you are," she whispers, her needles pausing mid-stitch. Her eyes are red-rimmed but dry, the kind of cried-out that comes after the tears have simply run their course. "Thought you were going to sleep through the whole week."

"How—" My voice comes out gravelly, making my hand go to my throat, but all I find is smooth skin. "How long?"

"Two days." Mother sets down her knitting and leans forward, pressing the back of her hand to my forehead in that instinctive, ageless gesture. "Strange faint, this was. You are not...with child, Elara. Are you?"

"No." It's a simpler answer than the truth of this entire ordeal. "I don't think so."

"Miss Hampshire nearly wore a trench in the floor with all her pacing." She glances at Vale beside me, her expression softening into something almost fond. "That husband of yours hasn't moved an inch. Slept through most of it, always holding, always keeping watch."

I look back at Vale. At the slow, easy rise of his chest beneath my hand. She doesn't know the half of it. It's better that way.

"He needed it," I murmur.

Mother hums, picking up her needles again. "I can see that. A man that tired has been carrying something heavy for a long, long while."

The clicking resumes. I watch her hands work, the wool sliding through her wrinkly, calloused fingers with practiced ease, and that's when I see it.

Her neck.

The dark veins, those black-purple threads that had spread beneath her skin like cracks in old plaster, are gone. Not faded. Gone. The skin there is smooth, a little loose with age as it should be, but clean. Untouched. As though the rot simply...retreated.

Something expands in my chest, hot and sudden and too big for the space it's in. I press my lips together to keep the sound inside, blinking hard against the sting in my eyes.

We did it. We broke the curse.

Mother catches my staring. "Noticed yesterday morning," she says quietly, her needles going still. "Thought it was a trick of the light at first. Checked again last night. And again this morning." She swallows, her jaw setting into that line I know so well, the one that means she's holding something enormous behind her teeth. "Palace rumor has it that the pestilence is retreating."

The door opens with the careful, practiced silence of someone who's spent decades moving through rooms without disturbing them. Miss Hampshire.

She enters carrying a tray with a steaming cup and a small bowl, takes one look at me, and stops. "Oh, thank the saints." The words leave her on an exhale, so relieved it sounds almost like a reprimand, as though my waking up is an inconvenience she's grateful for. She sets the tray down on the bedside table and straightens, smoothing her apron. "Two days, Your Majesty. I trust you will not make a habit of such theatrics."

"Wasn't planning on it." I push myself up against the pillows, careful not to jostle Vale, who hasn't so much as twitched. "How is...everything?"

"Everything is...righted." She produces a cloth from her apron and begins to polish the edge of the tray with the kind of focused aggression she usually reserves for dusty mantles. "The priests are clinging to the chapel floors in prayer, thanking God. And your husband..."

She glances at Vale's sleeping form with an expression caught between exasperation and respect.

"Still at it, I see." A click of her tongue. "Sleeping as

though he has no care in the world. As if there is suddenly less work to be done."

I look at her more carefully now. The angry red wound where her pustule had been is smaller, the inflamed edges pulling together with a tightness that speaks of healing rather than festering. The skin on her remaining fingers has lost that waxy, translucent quality, returning to something pink and alive.

Commotion drifts in from somewhere beyond the window. A murmur of voices layered over each other, hummed by a crowd that doesn't quite know the melody yet.

"What's that?"

"People," Miss Hampshire says as she crosses to the window and draws the curtain back. "Lining the gates to praise their queen."

Pale gold light floods the room, so warm and bright I have to squint. Through the glass, the courtyard is...alive. People move below, not in the shuffling, desperate way of the sick and starving, but with purpose. With energy.

"Folk from all over," Mother adds. "Been arriving since yesterday. Lining the palace walls with crocus flowers."

"Crocuses?"

"Reportedly, they have been pushing through the snow." Miss Hampshire turns from the window, and the light catches the sheen in her eyes. "All across the realm. Purple and yellow, breaking through the frost as if spring simply decided it had waited long enough."

The image settles into me like a hand pressed to a wound: the first real sign that this is over. Not the absence of rot on Mother's neck. But how the land itself is healing, remembering how to bloom.

My throat tightens. *Do you see this, Daron?*

I nod, not trusting my voice.

Miss Hampshire smooths the curtain back into place and turns with the brisk efficiency of a woman who won't linger on anything other than duty. "Your mother and I shall give you some privacy to wake properly. Broth is on the tray. You will drink it."

It's not a suggestion.

Mother rises, tucking her knitting into the chair with a final glance at Vale. "Rest, my child."

They leave together, the door clicking shut behind them with a soft finality that settles the room into a hush. Just the crackle of the hearth. The distant hum of voices beyond the window. And the slow, steady rhythm of Vale's breathing beneath my hand.

I ease back down against him, my cheek finding its place on his chest. My fingers trace the collar of his shirt, following the line to where the fabric parts and I can see the edge of his collarbone. Just warm, smooth skin and the steady proof of a heart that chose to feel everything rather than feel nothing.

I watch him for a long time.

The way his lashes rest against his cheeks. The way his lips part slightly on each exhale. The way one hand lies curled beside my hip, fingers loose and open as if, even in sleep, he's reaching for something.

I lift my hand to his jaw. Trace the line of it with my thumb. Lean in and press my lips to the corner of his mouth. "Vale..."

He stirs.

It's slow. A deep breath that expands his chest beneath me, followed by a languid tension that moves through his body like a cat stretching in a sunbeam. His hand finds my waist before his eyes find me, fingers tightening once, instinctively, pulling me closer before consciousness has fully arrived.

Then his lashes lift.

Green eyes, hazy with sleep, blink once. Twice. Settling on my face with the dazed, disoriented wonder of a man surfacing from a dream he didn't expect to have.

He stares at me. His hand leaves my waist and rises to my face, his thumb tracing beneath my eye as if checking that I'm real. That I'm solid. That I'm not the ghost his nightmares probably spent two days conjuring.

"You took your time," he says, his voice rough with sleep and hoarse with something deeper.

"I've been told I slept for two days." I press my cheek into his palm. "In my defense, someone slit my throat."

His jaw tightens. The humor doesn't quite land, the memory still too raw, too close. His thumb keeps moving beneath my eye, stroking as though the repetition is the only thing tethering him to the present.

"You almost didn't come back," he says quietly. The sleep haze has burned away, leaving something sharp and fragile in its wake. "I called for you. Over and over. And you just...kept drifting."

I just shrug. "Too comfortable with Death."

His jaw works. "I was beginning to think you'd fooled me after all. Got me to shatter the crown and break the curse, then decided to slip through into the light rather than stick it out with me."

A laugh catches in my throat, wet and unexpected. "Now that would've been a scheme worthy of a gravedigger."

He arches a brow. "It's not funny, Elara."

"A little, maybe?"

"No." His mouth curves anyway, slow and unsteady,

into the most genuine smile I've ever seen on him. "I don't know how to dig a grave properly, you saw so yourself." He lifts our joined hands and presses his lips to my fingers, lingering there. "If you'd stayed dead, I would've had to bury you myself, and it would've been a disgrace."

I bark out a laugh that scrapes my healing throat raw and makes me wince. "That's your concern? The craftsmanship of my burial?"

His eyes crinkle at the corners, and there it is again, that warmth, blooming slow and real through the green of his irises, so alive it makes my heart beat faster. "I missed you."

His arms tighten around me, pulling me back to rest on his chest. His lips press into my hair. And for a long, unhurried while, we simply lie there in the warmth of a sun-drenched room, listening to the hum of crocus-bearing crowds beyond the gate, the crackle of a hearth that burns instead of gutters, and the quiet, steady rhythm of a heart that finally, finally, beats whole.

TWENTY-THREE

Elara

Lavender drifts on the sun-warmed wool.

I lie on my back in the center of it, one arm behind my head, watching clouds drift across a sky so blue it feels like a personal affront to every gray, rot-choked morning the realm ever endured. Below the hill, fields stretch out in every direction—young stalks of grain pushing through dark soil in neat, green rows that ripple when the wind passes through them like fingers through hair.

Growing. All of it.

Vale sits beside me, his back propped against the trunk of an oak that's already flushed with new leaves, a spread of bread, cheese, and dried fruit arranged on a cloth between us. He tears a piece of bread and offers it to me without looking up from the view.

I shake my head, hand going to my stomach. "I'm not hungry."

"You haven't eaten since this morning."

"I had an apple."

"Half an apple." He turns the bread toward me again, brow arched. "The other half you fed to a horse that wasn't yours."

"She looked hungry," I say, waving the bread away.

Vale watches me for a moment, then sets the bread down and shifts closer, abandoning the food entirely. "If my wife won't eat," he murmurs, his hand finding the curve of my waist where my dress has ridden up just enough to bare a strip of skin, "then perhaps I shall."

His mouth finds my neck before I can roll my eyes.

"We're on a hill," I point out, though my voice has already gone thinner than I'd like. "In broad daylight. Anyone could—"

"The nearest farmstead is a mile south." His lips drag along the tendon of my throat, and I feel his smile against my pulse. "And I'm told the queen owns this land. Every blade of grass. Every inconveniently placed hill."

"That's not how land owner—" The protest dissolves into a sharp inhale as his teeth graze my collarbone. His hand slides from my waist to my hip, pulling me toward him across the blanket until my back is flush against his chest.

"I'm dizzy," I murmur.

"Dizzy bad?" he rasps, pressing a kiss to the hinge of my jaw. "Or dizzy good?"

"The verdict is not yet in."

"Then let me shift it toward good." His fingers finish with the laces, and the bodice loosens, letting the spring air slip against my skin. "I want—no, need you."

He takes his time peeling the fabric from my shoulders, his mouth following the path of each reveal—the curve of my shoulder, the ridge of my spine, the dip at the small of my back—with a patience that would be infuriating if it weren't so devastating.

I twist in his arms, finding his mouth with mine. The kiss is slow, tasting of bread and wine and the warm, unhurried ease of a man with nowhere to be. My fingers reach back to thread through his hair while his hands gather my skirts from behind, the linen rising in slow bunches until his palms find bare skin and the groan that leaves him vibrates against the nape of my neck.

He doesn't reposition me. Doesn't flip or pull or rearrange. He simply presses closer, his chest flush against my back, one arm sliding beneath me to band across my ribs while the other hooks my thigh, hitching it just enough. When he pushes inside from behind, the sound I make is swallowed by the open sky.

No damp walls to echo it back. No ceiling to contain it. Just the endless blue above and the steady, rolling rhythm of him filling me while the wind combs through the grass on every side.

He moves slowly. Each stroke is long and deliberate, a lazy, deep rocking of his hips that I feel all the way to my navel. The angle is different like this—tighter, fuller, the drag of him hitting places that make my fingers claw at the blanket beneath us. His mouth stays on my neck, my shoulder, the shell of my ear, breathing me in with each thrust as though I'm something he needs more than air.

"I keep worrying," he says between breaths, his lips grazing my ear, "that I'll wake up from all this sleeping I get to do now and find that this is just a dream. That I don't have a wife to do the most mundane, mortal things. Moment by moment."

"You're inside me," I pant, pressing back against him to meet his next stroke. "If this is a dream, then it's a good one."

He chuckles, a sincere sound that breaks his rhythm and buries itself warm and shaking against the curve of my neck. His grin curves against my skin, and something about that—Death laughing while fucking me on a sunlit hill—strikes me as so profoundly absurd that I laugh, too, breathless and bright, and for a moment, we're just two idiots tangled on a blanket, shaking with a joy that has no business existing, yet refuses to leave.

He finds his rhythm again, deeper now, his hand sliding from my thigh to my front. His fingers find the swollen heat between my legs, circling with the same unhurried patience he's brought to everything this afternoon, while his hips roll in long, devastating strokes that push the air from my lungs one thrust at a time.

The pressure builds in slow, cresting waves. His mouth on my neck. His fingers between my thighs. The thick fullness of him rocking into me from behind.

The orgasm doesn't crash so much as bloom. A long, shuddering unfurling that starts at his touch and radiates outward until my spine bows against his chest and his name leaves my mouth in a sound the fields can keep.

He follows with a low, guttural groan, his arm tightening around my ribs, pulling me flush against him as his hips stutter and press deep. I feel him pulse inside me, each throb heavy and warm, his forehead dropping to the curve of my shoulder while his breath comes apart in ragged, shaking pieces. We lie there after, breathing hard, the blanket twisted beneath us, the sun painting warmth across our tangled limbs.

A breeze passes over us, carrying the green smell of young grain and turned earth, and for a long, perfect moment there's nothing in the world but this.

"Well?" His lips move against my temple, lazy and smug. "How was that, hmm?"

My stomach flips.

Not the slow, unsettled queasiness from before. This is sharp. Sudden. A violent lurch that sends acid climbing my throat with no warning.

I shove him off me, roll sideways, and barely clear the edge of the blanket before my stomach empties itself into the wildflowers—half an apple included.

"That's..." Vale props himself on one elbow, watching me retch into a patch of crocuses. "Harsh judgment."

I spit, wiping my mouth on my sleeve, my eyes streaming. "It's not—" Another heave. I grip the grass until the wave passes, panting. "It's not you. Idiot."

He sits up, the smugness gone, replaced by genuine concern. His hand finds my back, rubbing slow circles between my shoulder blades. "Are you ill? Something you ate?"

"No, I don't think so." I sit back on my heels, dragging a shaky breath through my nose. The dizziness is receding, leaving behind a hollow, rinsed-out feeling and a strange, metallic taste on my tongue. "I was a little nauseous this morning. Fine on the ride here. Just now, only when I—"

I stop.

My hand has drifted to my belly without my permission, pressing flat against the soft plane beneath the rumpled linen. I look at Vale.

He's looking at my hand.

Looks up at me.

Hand. Me.

Neither of us breathes. Only the wind moves through the grass. A bird calls from the oak above. Below the hill, the young grain sways in its neat green rows, growing, growing, reaching for a sun that finally bothers to shine.

"Elara..." My name is barely a sound on his lips. "When was the last time you bled?"

"I don't...I don't remember." My palm presses flatter. "When we visited the lowlands? Before that? I...I don't know!" I all but mewl. "We were so busy with the constant traveling then."

"That was nearly two months ago..."

He stares at my stomach. I watch his face become a country at war with itself—borders shifting, defenses rising and crumbling in the same breath. Fear tightens the corners of his eyes. I know its shape on him by now: the way it locks his jaw, the way his shoulders brace as if against a blow.

But beneath it, something else is fighting to surface. Something bright and desperate, pushing against his ribs the way those crocuses pushed through frost.

His mouth opens. Closes. His breath comes in short, uneven pulls.

Then the fear cracks.

Not gone. Just...yielded to. Allowed to exist alongside the brighter thing rather than in place of it. His eyes go glassy. His jaw unclenches. And something I've never seen on his face before settles there: raw, trembling, terrified wonder.

His hand hovers over my belly. "May I?"

I nod.

His palm settles against my stomach. Broad. Warm. Trembling despite the steadiness of his arm. He holds it there, barely breathing, eyes fixed on the place where his hand meets my body as if he's listening for something too small to hear.

"I can't feel anything," he whispers.

"Vale... It would be the size of a seed," I say. "If it's anything at all."

"A seed." The word leaves him reverent and awed. He lowers himself slowly, carefully, until his lips press against my belly through the linen. The kiss is so soft I barely feel it, and yet it reaches somewhere so deep inside me that my eyes sting. "I didn't think it was possible." A shaky exhale against my belly. "After all these months, I thought...I thought perhaps Death simply couldn't."

A pause. A swallow. And quieter: "But here you are, little seed."

My hand finds his hair. I thread my fingers through the black curls and hold him there, against the place where something astonishing might be taking root inside the wife of Death.

Above us, the oak rustles. Below us, the fields stretch out in green and gold. And between us, on a sun-warmed blanket on a hill where nothing is rotting and everything is reaching for the light, the smallest, most terrifying, most extraordinary thing in the world begins.

TWENTY-FOUR

Death

Something is wrong with my wife.

The sensation hits mid-stride between realms—a sharp, jagged pull against my heartstrings that has nothing to do with a soul departing and everything to do with the one soul I can't bear to lose.

It yanks me sideways, dissolving the shadows I'm traveling through and stitching me back together in the palace hallway outside the royal chamber with enough force to crack the flagstone beneath my bony heel.

Miss Hampshire startles backward, her hand flying to her chest. "Saints alive!"

Of course, this woman recovers faster than most mortals would at the sight of a half-skeletal god materializing from thin air. Still, her complexion goes rather gray, probably because she's seen me one too many times throughout our past.

"What's happening?" I stride toward the double doors. "Is the baby coming?"

"Yes." Miss Hampshire steps into my path with the speed and precision of a woman who has spent decades blocking doorways from people far more intimidating than Death. Her nubs plant themselves flat against the oak. "But you are not going in there."

"I beg your pardon?"

"This is woman's work." Her chin lifts, her jaw set in that immovable line I've watched her deploy against ministers, priests, and at least one king. "You have no business being in that room."

A sound tears from my throat that rattles the sconces. "My wife is suffering through the birth of our first child. I will be at her side when she—"

"Looking like this? In your...evening attire?" Miss Hampshire gestures at me—at the exposed ribs, the skull, the cloak of living shadow pooling at my feet. "You'll send the maids into hysterics, and the midwife will drop the babe out of fright." She straightens her apron. "But that is beside the point. No king has ever been present for a birth. It is tradition."

"It was also tradition to slit queens' throats," I grind out, "and we seem to have moved past that."

Miss Hampshire opens her mouth. Closes it. Her eyes

narrow into slits so thin I'm genuinely impressed she can still see me through them.

I don't wait for her rebuttal.

The shadows swallow me whole for the briefest of seconds. Just long enough to weave bone into flesh, hollow sockets into green eyes, and ancient terror into the borrowed calm of Vale. Then I step through the door as though it isn't there at all...

...and straight into a battlefield.

Two maids scramble between the bed and a table laden with linens, hot water, and instruments I refuse to examine too closely. A stout midwife with rolled sleeves and an expression of seasoned authority kneels at the foot of the bed, her hands steady even as the woman in the bed is decidedly not.

Elara lies propped against a mountain of pillows, her shift soaked through, her hair plastered to her temples in dark, wet ropes. Violent red flushes her face, her teeth bared, her hands fisting the sheets with a grip that has turned her knuckles into white ridges.

I'm at her side in three strides, my hand finding hers. "I'm here."

"Oh, wonderful." The words come out in a snarl punctuated by a gasp that bows her spine off the pillows. "The man responsible for this finally shows up!"

I flinch at her shout. "I came as fast as I—"

"You came fast the night you put this child inside me, too, and look where that got us!"

One of the maids chokes on something that sounds suspiciously like a laugh. The midwife doesn't even blink. Presume this is the way of mortals and childbirth. One of many things I have yet to learn, to experience, so I borrow the stout woman's calm.

"You're doing beautifully," I murmur.

Elara crushes my fingers with a strength that would concern me if I weren't fairly certain I deserve it. "Nothing about this is *beautiful!* It feels like I'm being split apart by a...a battering ram wrapped in—oh god—"

Her words dissolve into a groan so guttural it vibrates through the bed frame. The midwife leans forward, murmuring instructions I can barely hear over the roaring in my skull.

Saints...maybe this is woman's work.

"Push now, Your Majesty," she says. "Bear down."

Elara bears down with a scream that could strip paint from walls. Her hand in mine becomes a vise, her nails biting crescents into my palm. "You're the worst husband alive."

A surreal chuckle tumbles from my lips. "You've called me worse."

"Breathe, Your Majesty," the midwife says, calm as a pond. "We're nearly there. One more."

"You said one more *three* one-mores ago!"

I brush the hair from her face with my free hand, wincing when another contraction hits and her grip threatens to rearrange the bones in my fingers. "Shh...you can do it."

"Push!" the midwife commands.

Elara, to my surprise, complies.

And the sound that leaves her is not a scream. It's something older, deeper. A sound that belongs to the beginning of things. Her body curves around the effort, every muscle drawn taut as a bowstring, her breath suspended in a moment that stretches so thin I'm convinced time itself halts for a moment.

Then...a cry.

Not Elara's.

Smaller. Sharper. A thin, furious wail that pierces the heavy air of the chamber and drives straight through my sternum like a lance of light.

"A girl!" The midwife lifts a slick, writhing, impossibly small creature into the light. "Healthy and whole, Your Majesty. A girl."

Elara collapses against the pillows, her chest heaving, tears streaming freely down her flushed cheeks. She's laughing. No, crying. No, laughing and crying all at once, her hand finally releasing mine to cover her mouth. All while the maids burst into motion.

I don't move.

I don't breathe.

Because the midwife rises with a bundle in her arms, so small it barely fills the crook of her elbow. She's holding it out to me as though this is ordinary, as though handing Death a new soul is something that happens every day.

"Your daughter, My Lord."

My arms lift on instinct, not thought. Pure instinct, ancient and bypassed by every rational function I possess. The midwife settles the bundle against my chest, and the weight of it—the devastating, negligible, impossible weight of it—stops my heart.

All three strings go still.

She's so small. A red, scrunched face no bigger than my palm, eyes squeezed shut against a world she's only just arrived in. Her mouth works in tiny, furious movements, lips pursing and unpursing as if she has inherited her mother's opinions but can't speak them yet.

But it's her aura that undoes me.

I've seen thousands of auras. Millions. The dim, flickering embers of the dying. The steady glow of the healthy.

The slow fade of the old. I know their vibrancy the way Elara knows the weight of soil.

This child blazes.

A light so bright and dense and ferociously alive that looking at it is like staring into a sun that hasn't learned how to set. Her entire body radiates with it, waves of luminance that pulse in time with a heartbeat so rapid it sounds like the wings of a hummingbird.

Fear arrives. Right on schedule, settling its familiar claws around my ribs with a grip I know too well. Because that blazing aura is finite. An hourglass. A number of grains I could count if I wanted to, each one a tick toward a silence I will one day have to witness.

My jaw locks. My arms tighten around the bundle.

Then she opens her eyes.

Dark. Unfocused. Blinking against the light with the confused, squinting displeasure of someone who was perfectly comfortable where they were, thank you very much.

She looks at me.

Not through me. Not past me. At me, with a directness that has no business belonging to a creature who is less than a minute old. Her tiny hand escapes the swaddling, fingers splaying wide before they curl around the edge of my collar and grip.

The fear cracks.

It crumbles because I cannot fathom an existence where this moment doesn't happen. A million years of solitude, of collecting souls in silence, of walking between worlds with nothing but shadows for company, and none of it, not a single second, was worth as much as the weight of this child in my arms.

I carry her to Elara.

My wife reaches for her with trembling, exhausted arms, and I lower our daughter into them with a care that borders on absurd for someone who has handled the dead for eternity. Elara cradles her against her chest, and the baby quiets instantly, her scrunched face smoothing into something closer to calm as she finds the warmth she was looking for.

"Oh..." Elara breathes, fresh tears tracking down her cheeks. "Oh, you're so angry."

"She has your temperament," I manage, though my voice comes out wrecked.

Elara looks up at me, her face blotchy and radiant and beautiful in a way that makes my chest feel like it's caving in. "Are you crying?"

I lift my hand to my face. My fingers come away wet. Not the liquid silver that has traced bone once before, but something simpler, warmer—human tears, from human eyes. Because whatever this feeling is, it's too mortal for a god to comprehend.

"For once," I whisper, sinking onto the edge of the bed, my hand finding the dark, downy crown of my daughter's head, "I didn't take a soul."

Elara's hand covers mine. "No."

"I helped create one." The words come out fractured, each one carrying more weight than the last, and I have to press my lips together to keep the rest of them from flooding out in a mess of incoherent awe. "I made...this."

"We made this," Elara corrects softly.

"Yes." I lower my head against her sweaty temple, leaving a kiss there before I whisper, "We should make more."

She chuckles. "Never again."

I look at my daughter. At the scrunched nose and the

angry brow and the tiny fist still clutching at nothing, demanding the world pay attention. At the blazing, impossible, finite aura that will one day dim and fade and go out.

And instead of grief, instead of the cold, preemptive mourning I braced myself for in graveyards and arguments and the long, dark hours before I chose this path, I feel something else entirely.

Gratitude.

Thankfulness for this single, unrepeatable, devastatingly brief moment. For the small weight of a life I helped make, resting against the chest of a woman I love, in a room filled with morning light and the distant sound of a realm that is learning, slowly and imperfectly, how to live again.

Now is all we're ever given.

I press my lips to my daughter's forehead. A kiss so soft it wouldn't disturb a petal.

Yes, I understand it now.

TWENTY-FIVE

Elara

Vale is staring at me again.

I can feel it the way you feel the sun on the side of your face: warm, persistent, entirely too focused for a man who should be watching his eldest daughter walk down the aisle. But no. He's gazing at the side of my head with the rapt attention of someone who's just discovered something extraordinary.

"What?" I whisper, keeping my eyes on the chapel doors where Maren is about to appear.

His fingers find the strand before I can stop him. He lifts it from behind my ear and holds it in the faint chapel light with the reverence of a man examining a relic.

"Another one," he murmurs, his mouth curving. "White like the bark of a birch."

"Put it back."

"I am not done admiring it."

"You're being strange."

"I'm being mesmerized." He tucks the strand back into place, his fingertips lingering at my temple, tracing the fine lines that fan out from the corner of my eye. "Do you know what these are?"

"Wrinkles, Vale. They're *wrinkles*."

"Evidence," he corrects softly, his thumb following a crease that deepens when I squint. "That you laughed too hard at supper last week. That you frown in your sleep." His touch drifts to the corner of my mouth, where the skin creases more than it once did. "That you've spent twenty years smiling at me when I don't deserve it."

Something warm and familiar turns over in my chest. He does this often, mapping the changes in my face with a tenderness that should feel humbling and instead feels like worship. Every new line, every shift in the landscape of my body, he discovers and registers as though it's a gift being unwrapped slowly over decades.

The elongated, pale lines on my hips from three pregnancies? He traces them in bed like roads on a map, asking which child left which one. The silver in my hair? He finds each new strand with the delight of a boy finding coins in a fountain. The softness that settled around my waist after our youngest? He wraps his arms around it every night as though it's the only shape he ever wanted to hold.

My husband looks at me as though I'm the most exquisite thing he's ever seen. "Extraordinary."

"You're missing the wedding," I murmur, nodding toward the altar.

"I'm attending the wedding. I'm simply prioritizing which view deserves my attention right now."

"How does the queen's husband still look so young?" murmurs some lady in a pew behind us. "Must be years of good living."

I press my lips together to smother the laugh that threatens to ruin the ceremony. If only the woman knew what climbs into bed beside me every night. What comes out when the doors are locked and the family is shut away from gossip and minds that couldn't fathom how the Reign of Rot ended.

Granted, having a perpetually handsome husband during official events has its benefits. Even if the truth behind the glamor would send the entire chapel screaming into the courtyard.

On Vale's lap, Edmund fusses.

Our youngest is barely two. A late and deeply unexpected addition who arrived with the same furious wail as his sister and has maintained that volume ever since. He squirms against Vale's chest, one chubby fist tangling in the collar of his father's forest-green vest.

"Shh." Vale bounces him with the practiced, absent rhythm of a man who has done this three times now and still hasn't quite mastered it.

Edmund responds by shoving his fingers into Vale's mouth. "Papa, leave!"

Vale removes the chubby fingers with the dignity of a god being publicly humiliated by a toddler. "Your son is bored."

"He's your son when he's difficult."

"He's always difficult."

"Wonder where he gets that from…"

Vale rolls his eyes. "Oh, I know the answer to that."

Beside me, Rowan shifts in his seat. Eighteen, tall, dark-haired like his father but built like my side of the family—broad-shouldered, sturdy, the frame of a young man who spent his childhood helping the groundskeeper dig fence posts and haul stone. He doesn't fidget out of boredom. He fidgets because sitting still in formal clothes makes him itch, and I know this because I still feel this way after two decades of being queen.

He'll be king one day.

Not that Maren couldn't be queen; she certainly could. Brilliantly so, and everyone knows it. But when the question was put to her at sixteen, my eldest daughter looked at the uncursed, perfectly normal crown on my head, looked at me, and said, "No, thank you. I've seen what that thing does to a person's privacy."

And so…it falls to Rowan. Kind. Steady. Occasionally too earnest for his own good—qualities that will make him a great king, I'm sure of it.

"Stop fidgeting," I murmur, nudging his shoulder.

He straightens, tugging at his collar. "The lace is itchy."

"Rough cotton is worse." I keep my voice low, my eyes on the altar where the priest is arranging candles. "Your grandfather shoveled dirt for a living, Rowan. Your grandmother still knits her own stockings. Where we come from, nothing was given. Everything was dug out of the ground with blistered hands. They ache for days, whereas the lace will only itch for another hour."

Rowan glances at me, the fidgeting pausing. He has

Vale's eyes—that sharp, searching green—but the way he listens is all his father's, too. Bored after all, perhaps.

"Once you wear that crown," I continue, "you remember the people who dig. The ones who shovel and haul and bury their dead with shaking hands. Their hardships. The dirt they stand in."

"Like you did," he says low.

"Like I still do." My mouth curves. "I still know my way around a grave. Though my knees have strong opinions about it now."

Rowan smiles. A small, real thing that softens the serious set of his jaw. "And if I forget?"

I lean closer, bumping my shoulder against his. "Then your father will remind you. Death runs in this family, Rowan. He'll never let you forget."

His gaze drifts to Vale, who is currently extracting Edmund's fingers from his nose with an expression of regal suffering. Something warm and knowing passes through Rowan's eyes.

He doesn't flinch at the reference—none of our children do. They grew up with a father who sometimes forgot to wear his human face at the breakfast table, who occasionally walked through walls when he was distracted, and who once terrified a palace cook so badly she quit on the spot when he materialized in the pantry looking for biscuits.

They know what he is.

They love him dearly.

Perhaps that's his greatest lesson, even more than mine. That the thing the world fears most can sit in a chapel pew, bouncing a toddler on his knee, crying at his daughter's wedding, and still be the best father I've ever seen.

The doors open.

Maren steps through.

Ivory silk wraps her, simple and clean, her dark hair pinned in the same practical twist I wore the day I married her father. No jewels. No elaborate braids. Just Maren, plain and simple.

Beside me, Vale goes still, wearing an expression so full it could flood the chapel. His hand finds mine on the pew between us. His fingers lace through mine—warm, steady, trembling just slightly—and squeeze.

I squeeze back.

"She's so beautiful," he whispers, his voice cracking at the seams. "She looks like you." He turns to take me in, and the green of his eyes is bright, impossibly bright, swimming with decades of moments exactly like this one. "Thank you."

"What for?"

His thumb traces across my knuckle, slow and deliberate, the way he's done a thousand times in a thousand quiet moments across twenty years. "For making me choose this."

The organ swells. Maren reaches the altar. Edmund shrieks with delight at something only toddlers can see, and Rowan leans forward in his seat, watching his sister with the quiet, steady attention of a boy who's already learning how to hold the weight of things that matter.

I rest my head against Vale's shoulder and watch our daughter begin her life. This. All of this. *The perfect happy ending.*

Worth every grain of sand.

TWENTY-SIX

Death

Golden light pours through the open windows of the royal chamber, pooling on the quilt, warming the thin hands that rest on top of it. Her hands. When did they become so frail?

The knuckles are prominent now, the veins raised beneath papery skin. They don't look like the hands that once gripped a shovel for hours, or clawed at my cloak, or held our firstborn against her chest.

And yet they are. Every line, every age spot, every creak

in the joints is a record of something she touched, something she held, something she refused to let go of.

I hold one of them now. My skeletal thumb traces across her knuckles with the same slow rhythm I used to comb through her hair all those mornings ago. The skin is looser than it was. Softer. I could map the years across it like a cartographer, pinpointing the exact ridge where she gripped the reins too hard the winter Edmund was born, the small scar on her index finger from a pruning knife in Queen Maeryn's greenhouse.

I look at her dimming aura.

One-thousand-two.

One-thousand-one.

It's not the guttering fade of the sick or the sudden snuffing of the young. This is gentler. A candle burning low in a room where it's been burning for a long, long time, the flame still steady, still warm, just...quieter. Smaller. Finding its way to the bottom of the wick with a grace that most mortals don't get.

She's not in pain; I've made certain of that—the only nudge she allowed me, a slight easing of the body's last tensions, smoothing the rough edges of the passage the way one might polish glass so the grains won't catch.

"You're staring again," she rasps, her voice thin as old parchment.

"Admiring." My thumb continues its circuit. "There's a difference."

Her mouth curves. Weak, but real. Even now, even at the bottom of the wick, she smiles at me the way she always has. Like I'm ridiculous, and she's chosen to find it endearing rather than insufferable.

The children are here. All of them.

Maren stands at the foot of the bed, her arms wrapped

around herself, her dark hair streaked with silver at forty. She has her mother's pragmatism and my stubbornness, and she's not crying. Not yet. She's holding it the way Elara taught her: steady, with both hands, until the job is done.

Rowan sits on Elara's other side, his broad hand covering hers on the quilt. He grew into the crown the way trees grow into the shapes the wind gives them. He's been a good king. The sort who stands in the dirt with the people who dig, just as his mother asked.

Edmund sits cross-legged on the floor with his two-year-old daughter asleep in his lap, bouncing his knee with a restless energy that reminds me so much of my mortal form I have to look away for a moment. His wife stands behind him, one hand on his shoulder.

Maren's three children—twin boys of twelve, and a girl of eight—sit in a row on the window seat, legs dangling, watching with wide, solemn eyes.

"Grammy," the girl whispers, tugging at her mother's sleeve. "Why is Grandfather all bony today?"

I look at the child, and the softness that moves through my chest is a physical thing, pressing against all three strings. "Your grandmother likes me best this way."

"Only confirms my taste is terrible," Elara rasps from the pillows.

Laughter ripples through the room. It's fragile, precious. It's very much how our family handles death—like a welcome relative that lives alongside us until the last kernel falls.

They say their goodbyes one by one. I watch each of them approach, lean in, and try to fold a lifetime of love into a single kiss on a weathered cheek.

Maren goes first, pressing her lips to Elara's forehead

and lingers there, her fingers curling into the quilt. "Thank you," she whispers. "For everything."

"You would've been a wonderful queen," Elara murmurs.

Maren pulls back, eyes bright and swimming. "I know. That's why I had the good sense to decline."

She gathers her children. The eight-year-old waves at Elara from the doorway, small and uncertain, and Elara lifts her trembling fingers to wave back, and the effort it costs her hits me like a blade between the ribs.

Edmund kneels beside the bed next. He doesn't speak for a long time. Just looks at his mother, his eyes the color of mine, and presses his forehead to her hand.

"I'll be loud enough for both of us," he finally manages.

"You always have been." Her fingers find his hair. "Take care of your sister."

"Maren doesn't need taking care of."

"I know. Do it anyway."

He kisses her knuckles and leaves without looking back. I know why. Edmund breaks in private, and I will find him later—a father's hand on a grieving son's shoulder, away from witnesses.

Rowan is last.

He sits there holding her hand, running his thumb over the same knuckles I've been tracing, trying to assemble words big enough for what he feels. I know the futility of that search. I've been practicing it for years and have come up empty every time.

"You'll be fine," Elara tells him.

"I know."

"The realm is in good hands."

"I know." His voice cracks. He clears his throat, squares

his shoulders in that way he does when he's pretending. "Death runs in the family. I remember."

He presses his cheek to hers for several breaths, then stands. He looks at me. Something passes between us that doesn't require language—the understanding of two men who love the same woman and know that one of them must leave the room now.

My son nods. I nod back.

The door closes. The room exhales.

Just us.

Death and his gravedigger wife.

The quiet that settles is the kind she's always loved best —the hush after a burial, when the dirt is patted down and the mourners have gone. My thumb resumes its slow circuit, and the candlelight flickers against my bones.

"Find any new wrinkles?" she whispers.

"Several." I lift my bony finger to her face, tracing the deep lines that bracket her mouth, the creases at her eyes, the papery softness of her cheek. "They're magnificent."

"Liar."

"Never. Not about this." I trace the crease at the corner of her eye. "This one is from the day Edmund put a frog in Maren's bed. You laughed so hard you couldn't breathe." My finger moves to the line between her brows. "This one is from the trade negotiations with the southern provinces. Three weeks of frowning." Down to the bracket beside her mouth. "And this one...this one is mine. Decades of sharing in joy and laughter with me."

Her eyes glisten. "You deserved most of them."

"Debatable."

We're quiet for a while. The sun sinks lower, turning the gold to amber. Her breaths are coming slower now, with longer pauses between them, each one a deliberate act.

Each pause quiets my strings, a suspension, the terrible anticipation of a silence that will eventually hold. "Oh, Elara…"

She trundles up an exhausted smile, hair that has gone completely white framing her age-speckled face. "I'm not afraid."

My eye sockets burn. "I know."

"It feels like it did before… In the throne room." Her eyes close for a moment. "Like coming home."

My jaw clenches so hard the bone creaks. "I will forever be your home."

"Then stop being sad."

"Impossible request." My voice fractures. I bring her hand to my mouth—to the side that's still lips—and press it there. "Denied."

A breath of laughter, so thin it's barely air. "Worst husband."

"Best wife." I lower my forehead to hers. Bone to skin. One last time. "The best thing that ever happened to the worst thing in existence."

Her hand rises slowly, with effort that costs her too much, and lays flat against my open chest. Three heart-strings hum against her palm. The same palm that first reached into my ribcage in a moonlit clearing and told me my heart was healing.

"Take care of them," she whispers. "All of them."

"With everything I am."

"And yourself."

A sound leaves me that isn't quite a laugh. "That, I cannot promise."

"Live." Her fingers curl weakly against my ribs. "For them…and for me."

I nod. A single dip of my skull that she feels against her

forehead rather than sees, because her eyes are closing now, the gold around us dimming in a way that has nothing to do with the sun.

"Elara." I say her name the way I said it in the throne room. Like a prayer. Like the first and last word in a language only we speak. "Say it. One more time."

"I love you." The words come as easily as they did the first time. Easier, maybe, shaped by years of practice. "I'll love you even after this."

My voice is a ruin. "And I'll love you until the day I die."

Her aura dims.

Dims more.

The candle finds the bottom of its wick, and the flame doesn't dance or fight. It simply softens, glowing warm and amber and perfectly still, before it eases itself out with the quiet dignity of a woman who spent her whole life among the dead and was never once afraid of joining them.

Her soul passes through me.

It's not like the others. Not the brief, anonymous transit of a stranger's light being carried to rest. Hers presses against my heartstrings. Warm. Deliberate. Lingering. As if she's running her hand along them one last time, checking her work. Making sure the mending holds.

Oh, it holds.

It hurts.

It's a devastating hurt as she expands into the vast, peaceful stillness where all souls go, and the warmth goes with her, and the room is quiet, and my wife is gone.

I should stand. Should open the door. Should let the children in, let the grief be shared the way grief must be shared.

Instead, I fold forward until my skull rests against the quilt beside her hip. The sound that tears from my chest has no word, no name. It rips through three whole heart-strings with enough force to shred them, but they don't. They hold. They hold because she made them hold, because she mended them with stubbornness and snowballs and the infuriating, magnificent insistence that love is worth the price.

I grip her hand and press it to my jaw, to my teeth, to the bone she once traced with fearless, curious fingers in a moonlit clearing when she could have screamed and didn't. Tears streak down my skull—not gold, not silver—just salt and water and grief, pooling in the hollows of my sockets before spilling over in dark, spreading circles on the quilt.

"Gone for a minute, and I already miss you so much," I choke out, speaking to a body that no longer holds my wife. "How am I supposed to live without you, hmm?"

The room doesn't answer. The candles gutter. The sun has gone, leaving only the deep blue of twilight and the persistent, aching hum of three heartstrings that refuse to break.

I weep until there's nothing left. Until my rib bones ache and my throat is raw tendons and the only sound is the creak of my bones as I breathe. Then I lift my head and look at her face: peaceful, smooth, the lines I loved softened by the particular gentleness that only death can offer.

I press my lips to her forehead.

Stand.

Open the door.

They're waiting. Maren with her arms around her brothers. Rowan with his jaw set in his mother's line. Edmund with red-rimmed eyes and a sleeping toddler against his shoulder. They look at me—at the tear-streaked skull, at the god who just lost the only thing that ever made eternity bearable—and they don't flinch.

Maren steps forward. She wraps her arms around my ribcage, around the bones and shadow and the broken, beating heart inside, and holds on.

Then Rowan. Then Edmund, toddler and all.

I stand in the hallway with my children's arms around me, my wife's soul resting in the stillness of everything.

And my family holds me.

CHAPTER

TWENTY-SEVEN

Death

"You're hovering."

"I don't hover," I say. "I *loom*. There's a distinction."

"Loom quieter, then. You're making the nurses question their life choices."

She doesn't look up from the instruments she's arranging on the tray. Her hands move with a precise, unhurried efficiency I've watched in this bloodline for generations, though each pair of hands is somehow new, somehow hers in a way that still catches me off guard.

242

Her name is Sera. Great-great-great-granddaughter of Rowan, which makes her—I've long since lost count of the greats—mine. She has Edmund's stubbornness. Maren's jaw. Dark hair pinned in the same practical twist her ancestors have worn for generations, as though the women of this line agreed long ago that vanity is a luxury best left to people with less important things to do.

But her mouth...

That sharp, blunt, takes-no-prisoners mouth that is currently terrorizing the head nurse into a very small corner of the room.

That's Elara's.

They all carry a piece of her. A gesture here, a tilt of the head there. The way they frown when thinking, or laugh too loudly in quiet rooms, or dig their heels in on arguments they've already won. I find her scattered through all of them, refracted like light through a prism—each fragment different, each unmistakably from the same source.

Sera is the brightest fragment in decades.

"Stop staring at me like that." She snaps a cloth tight between her hands and lays it across the swollen belly of the woman on the table. "It's unsettling."

"I'm not staring. I'm admiring."

Her eyes flick to mine. Brown, not green, but sharp enough to cut and narrow. "You say that to every woman in this family."

"I mean it every time."

She makes a sound that is not quite a scoff and not quite a laugh, which is also Elara's. "Right. Tell me her aura."

I look at the woman on the table. She's been laboring for nine hours, the child inside her turned wrong. Three midwives tried everything before someone rode for Sera, who arrived with her leather case of instruments and her scandalous theories about surgery and her very specific request that her "uncle" accompany her.

Uncle works under most circumstances. Our family line abandoned trying to explain me to outsiders sometime around the third generation.

"Her aura is strained," I say. "Flickering at the edges. The child's is separate. I can distinguish it now."

"That's good." She reaches for a blade so clean and precise it looks nothing like the ceremonial knives of the old histories.

"Or bad. Depending on what you do next." I pause. "What exactly are you planning to do with that?"

"Cut her open." She says this the way one might announce the weather. "Remove the child through the abdomen. Stitch everything back together." She positions herself at the foot of the table. "It works. I've done it eleven times successfully."

"And the other times?"

"Two." A beat. "They were a long time ago, and I've improved considerably." She glances up at me. "Don't give me that look."

"I'm not giving you a look."

"You're giving me the look my great-however-many-grandmother described in her diary. The one that apparently means *I find this simultaneously impressive and profoundly alarming.*"

She kept diaries. Of course she kept diaries. And of course, Sera read them. "She was an accurate writer."

"She was." Something softens briefly in Sera's expression, like a candle flame in a draft—there, then steadied. "Right. When I cut, I need you to narrate every shift in the aura. Brighter, dimmer, which direction. Specifically."

"I'm aware of how auras function. I've been reading them since before your kind discovered fire."

"And I've been performing surgery since before you discovered that hovering over a patient is unhelpful." She doesn't look up. "So we're both operating outside our comfort. Ready?"

"Proceed."

The blade descends.

I watch the woman's aura as Sera works, calling the shifts the way a sailor calls the wind. "Steady. Dimming—hold. Stabilizing."

"Good?"

"Relatively."

"'Relatively' is not a medical term."

"Neither is 'cut her open and stitch it back together,' yet here we are." I pause. "She's stabilizing. Continue."

Sera continues. Her hands move with a confidence that borders on defiance, each cut deliberate, each stitch placed with the grim precision of a woman who has decided that losing patients to me is an insult she will not tolerate.

"The child's aura is very bright," I offer. "Impatient."

"Runs in the family."

"Oh?" Another glance at the mother. "Are we related?"

"A dozen times removed."

"I'm losing count..." Presume that is also a mortal conundrum.

Sera reaches deeper as the woman's light flickers toward the familiar pull of my own nature—the endless gravity of what I am. "Aura?"

"Dimming."

Sera's jaw tightens. That jaw. "How much?"

"Enough to concern me."

"You're Death. You're not supposed to be concerned; you're supposed to be pleased."

"I find I've developed opinions about which souls come to me and when." I move to the woman's side and take her free hand, the one not gripping the table edge. She can't fully comprehend me in her state, but she senses the steadying weight of something vast pressing gently against the fraying edges of her light. "Stay," I tell her. "Your child is almost here. Stay a moment longer."

Her fingers close around mine.

"Talking to her?" Sera asks, not looking up. "Fighting death?"

"Apparently."

"Is it working?"

"Her grip just tightened."

"Good. Keep going."

"I wasn't aware I took instructions from—"

"Uncle..." The word is quiet. Pointed. And beneath it, something unguarded. A flicker of the thing she refuses to show in front of the nurses. Fear. Not of failure. But of this specific loss, in this specific room, with this specific witness. "Please."

I keep talking. Low, unhurried, the kind of voice I used once beside a boy's cot in an orphanage, beside a young king in a throne room, beside a gravedigger's deathbed. The voice that isn't mine and has always been mine—the part of Death that learned, very late, to hold on as well as to let go.

"There!" Sera's hands go in and lift.

The child emerges. Slick. Furious. Already deeply inconvenienced by the world, the sound he makes piercing the chamber like a lance of light.

The aura blazes.

I release the mother's hand. Her light is stabilizing: flickering still, but catching, the way a flame sputters before it commits to the wick.

She'll live.

Sera cleans the child with efficient hands that betray only the faintest tremor and lowers him to his mother's chest. "A boy. Healthy and whole."

The mother's sob is the sound of relief so total it breaks the body a little on its way out. Her arms curl around the bundle with the ancient, instinctive grip I've watched a thousand times.

Sera strips off her gloves. Turns to me. The professional composure is mostly intact except at the edges, where something bright and fierce and desperately controlled is fighting its way through.

"Well?" she asks. "Both auras?"

"The child is blazing." A pause. "The mother will live."

One sharp nod. A crack at its edges, letting through one unguarded flash of raw triumph before she buries it. She turns away, busying herself with instruments that don't need attention, and I watch the set of her shoulders as she breathes through whatever is happening inside her chest.

So like her.

I never say it. But I feel it in the strings—that quiet, resonant ache that moves through me whenever one of them walks through the world the way Elara would have loved. The stubbornness. The competence. The absolute refusal to let death have the last laugh.

After a moment, Sera speaks, her back still to me, her voice carefully level. "You know," she says, "my colleagues think I'm unhinged. Requesting my ancient, mysterious uncle attend surgeries."

"Are they wrong?"

"About the unhinged part? Probably not." A beat. "But having Death in the room does statistically improve outcomes."

"I've never given you favorable statistics."

"No. You just stand there looking grim, and everyone tries harder." She turns, finally, and the composure has been reassembled. Nearly perfect, except for the brightness still sitting in her eyes. "You're very motivating. As a specter of inevitable doom."

"Highest compliment I've received in decades."

Her mouth curves. That mouth. "Gran wrote about that, too," she says quietly. "That you were funny. That she didn't expect it."

The strings hum. "She told everyone who would listen."

"I know. I've read every word she left." Sera looks down at the clean instruments in her hands, then back up at me. "She said the funniest thing about Death was that he kept choosing to show up." A pause. "I think she meant it as a love letter."

The room is very quiet.

"She meant everything as something," I say, which is not adequate, but is the most I can manage with three heartstrings pulling at once.

Sera nods. Just once. Then she turns back to the mother and child, slipping back into the precise, unhurried competence of a woman with more work to do.

I look at the boy in his mother's arms. At the blazing, impossible, finite aura that will one day dim. And one day, I will carry this soul, too—the way I've carried so many, the way I'll carry all of them, every last descendant of a gravedigger who once lay down in a hole in the earth and dared Death to come find her.

But not today.

Today, Death helped bring a child into the world. Today, my bloodline stood over a table with steady hands and a sharp mouth and pulled life from the jaws of the very thing I am.

I used to fear this. An unending succession of losses. An infinite lineage of goodbyes. Every hello carries its goodbye folded inside it, like a letter you know you'll have to open someday.

But hello comes first.

An endless succession of life, of love.

Of *now*.

THIS CONCLUDES *Crown Me Yours*. If you have a moment, please consider leaving my story a review.

What an ending, huh? Wanna talk about it? Join me in my Facebook Reading Group for free group therapy as we discuss this series.

CONNECT WITH ME! (NO REALLY, PLEASE DO!)

Join my mailing list and get access to my VIP Lounge, exclusive illustrations, bonus chapters, and news about my stories. Email Sign Up